DATE DUE

OC 11 '00			
OC 10			
GAYLORD			PRINTED IN U S A

The Moves Make The Man

THE MOVES MAKE THE MAN

A NOVEL BY

Bruce Brooks

CORNERSTONE BOOKS

ABC-CLIO

Santa Barbara, California
Oxford, England

First published 1984 in the United States by Harper & Row, Publishers, Inc. and in Great Britain 1988 by Pan Books, Limited.

Published in Large Print 1988 by arrangement with Harper & Row, Publishers, Inc. and Pan Books, Limited.

Cover illustration © 1984 by Wayne Winfield.

Library of Congress Cataloging-in-Publication Data

Brooks, Bruce.
  The moves make the man / Bruce Brooks.
    p. cm.
  "Cornerstone books."
  Summary: A Black boy and an emotionally troubled white boy in North Carolina form a precarious friendship.
    ISBN 1–55736–048–0 (lg. print): $14.95 (est.)
    1. Large type books. [1. Afro-Americans—Fiction.
2. Emotional problems—Fiction. 3. Friendship—Fiction.
4. Large type books.] I. Title.
[PZ7.B7913Mo 1988]   [Fic]—dc19   87–30717
                                         CIP AC

10 9 8 7 6 5 4 3 2 1

ABC-Clio, Inc.
2040 Alameda Padre Serra
Santa Barbara, California 93103-1788

Clio Press Ltd.
55 St. Thomas' Street
Oxford, OX1 1JG, England

This book is smyth-sewn and printed on acid-free paper ∞.
Manufactured in the United States of America.

For Penelope and Alexander,
and the clans of Brooks, Collins, and Hunt

The author gratefully acknowledges the James A. Michener Fiction Award he received from the Iowa Writers' Workshop during the writing of this novel, and the inspiration he received from: Earl Monroe, Roland Hanna, Henry Beetle Hough, Don Dixon, and Declan McManus.

FIRST PART

1.

Now, Bix Rivers has disappeared, and who do you think is going to tell his story but me? Maybe his stepfather? Man, that dude does not know Bix deep and now he never will, will he? Only thing he could say is he's probably secretly happy Bix ran away and got out of his life, but he won't tell you even that on account of he's busy getting sympathy dumped on him all over town as the poor deserted guardian.

How about Bix's momma? Can she tell you? I reckon not—she is crazy in the hospital. And you can believe, they don't let crazies have anything sharp like a pencil, else she poke out her eye or worse. So she won't be writing any stories for a long time. But me—I have plenty of pencils, number threes all sharp and dark green enamel on the outside, and I have four black and white marble composition books. Plus I can tell you some things, like Bix was thirteen last birthday (same as

me), Bix was a shortstop (supreme), Bix
gets red spots the size of a quarter on his
cheekbones when angry and a splotch
looks like a cardinal smack in the middle
of his forehead when he is ashamed. I can
tell a lot more besides, including why Bix
ran away. You just listen to me and you'll
be getting the story, all you want. You
don't pay any mind to all this creepy jive
that is going around town and school now
about how Bix was bad and crazy like his
momma and deserted her when she was
sick and his stepfather too. Didn't I hear
that old snooty preacher at the white First
Baptist saying so last Sunday, moaning
about children full of sin, with everybody
in the church mooning with sympathy and
staring all mushy over at the poor stepfather sitting in the third row?

I went by there to talk to that man after
church, thinking to catch him all softened
up and ask had he got any word of Bix.
But when I heard that sin-child chatter, I
gave it over. Fact I almost jumped right
into their high service mumbo and told
them what they were about—that would
have been a sight, this skinny kid black as
a clarinet wailing out a licorice tune right
there on the light blue carpet aisle cutting
off that organ with the fake pipes just as it
wheezed into one of their wavery old
hymns. But it would not have done ary bit

of good. When people are set to hear bad things, that is what they will hear. Listen, that is just about all white people go to church for, to have some soft old duck moan at them about all the sins ever been committed and all going to keep right on being committed so we might just as well give up on getting good, and settle for getting a nasty thrill watching the sins go on. You don't hear that kind of giving up at the colored churches around here, I can tell you. People mostly go there to sing, which is different from moaning any day.

When I came home from that church I was angry at the lies being told. Not just that they told that Bix was bad and a runaway—because there was some bad growing in Bix, and he did run away and that is that. But those people did not understand worth a penny.

That is when and why I decided to write this story of Bix. Of Bix and me, mostly, I guess it has to be. I may not understand it all yet myself, but I got all summer ahead of me, and a room to myself, cool up under the eaves, because my brother Henri is off to camp. My momma wanted to send me first, but I told her I wouldn't go on account of I knew I could use the summer better writing this out. So it's Henri gets to make the wallets and lanyards and sing the national anthem while the flag is

raised every morning and swim in a lake
warm as blood.

It's me gets to tell the truth.

2.

Something else is, I have Bix's notebook.

Now, Bix was not a great writer like me. I got seven straight grades of all A in English, six in black schools that were harder than the white one, which nobody believes. The lunches were better at the colored schools too, but nobody buys that either. Anyway, Bix is about B- in English and bad handwriting to boot. But he did keep a notebook.

Mostly the book is full of study on how to play the position of shortstop in baseball. Bix wrote down all kinds of things he heard or thought about playing double-s, including fourteen pages all the way to the margin written fast as fire, taking down word for word a special radio show where Phil Rizzuto talked for half an hour straight on the fine points of the job. Looks like that Rizzuto can motor the mouth, because he left Bix in the dust several times and there is nothing to show but these dots (. . .) for these spots. There is one other funny thing. One of the fine points Rizzuto allows is that A shortstop has to spin light. This is nothing hard to figure, since the shortstop turns the pivot on double plays, though it is a pretty phrase. But it went straight to Bix's head and spun HIM, because the next page after the Rizzuto interview is covered with nothing but repetitions of the words SPIN LIGHT SPIN LIGHT SPIN LIGHT SPIN LIGHT. Then at the bottom is one sentence: I WILL PLAY MY GAME BENEATH THE SPIN LIGHT.

The rest of the notebook is recipes and notes for taking care of your baseball glove. Really, recipes. There are three pages telling how to make homemade hickory ash ointment for heel flex, and a chart showing the seven places where you just got to stick balsam paste if you want your glove to do something called HOLD MAXIMAL HINGE LINE. I knew this stuff was in the book, for Bix told me about it a few weeks ago when I watched him fix his glove with these very things.

As soon as I decided to write this story I knew I had to have this notebook. Bix had told me he kept it in his comic collection, between GREEN LANTERN and the JUSTICE LEAGUE OF AMERICA.

I knew his stepfather would not give it to me if I asked. And anyway it was between

Bix and me. So last night I got out of bed at midnight and snuck off my roof, which I could never have done if Henri was still here because he sleeps like a dog with one eye open. I had on my high black Chucks for grip, and a black sweater and blue jeans.

I snuck on over to Bix's old house. It was dark. I knew his stepfather slept downstairs in the back of the house, so I was not worried about him. I also knew Bix's room was on the second floor, right in front. So I climbed the porch railing and up onto the ridge of the decoration above the door, and then grabbed the sill of Bix's old window and pulled myself up, tennies gripping the brick just fine. I picked the window open pretty quietly with a grapefruit knife and raised it and climbed right on in.

For a minute I just stood there getting sad. That room had a smell that was like Bix, something like leaves on the ground but like fresh dough too. In the moonlight that came in slanty through the window I could see Bix's baseball cap on the post of a chair and a pair of his tennies, one of them in the seat of that chair and the other on its side underneath. There were newspaper clippings on the walls and I could read the big black letters of one of them where the moon hit: McCOVEY SMASH CAUGHT— YANKS TAKE SERIES. I could even barely smell Bix's old baseball glove somewhere nearby. As I say, I watched him oil it up this spring and he explained you could smell if a glove was oiled the right way and made me sniff it before and after he worked it in.

Even though I had never seen it when it was his I could tell it was not Bix's room any longer. The sheets were stripped off the mattress, and the big flat ugly thing looked weird and like it had never touched a human in all its days, with these aqua stripes and a couple of large labels sewn on and this roping around the edges. A bed without sheets is one of the ugliest things you ever see. Also there were some boxes piled inside the door, and I knew they were for Bix's stuff to get piled into. I found the comics collection, in a large old box under the back window. I looked up the GREEN LANTERNs and there was the notebook. It is a red spiral one. Personally I hate the spiral kind. Bix liked it because he could keep his pencil inside the spiral. I keep my pencil behind my ear. You may want to write something down and not always have the notebook handy, but Bix of course was not a writer and probably never did.

I tucked the notebook inside my shirt and walked back over to the window to leave. But then I saw Bix's glove, tossed in the front corner of the room, and you know I had to pick it up and sniff it and then I couldn't help it but started to cry, first time

I ever cried about Bix, feeling like I had lost something and then feeling like I did not know if I ever had it. Bix was gone and worse the Bix I used to dig was gone even before he went and I didn't know where either of them was but he left his glove behind, which he must be unhappy without regardless of being the old Bix or the new. When I smelled the glove I could tell it was oiled the right way. I chucked it back in the corner and climbed out.

I came down much as I went up, only jumping all the way from the decoration over the door instead of climbing onto the railing. That wooden thing in the middle of the decoration is a pineapple, which I never could tell before. Why put a wooden pineapple up over a door?

I got back to my room okay. I stayed up pretty late reading the whole notebook, reading every single repetition of SPIN LIGHT SPIN LIGHT SPIN LIGHT until it meant all these different things to me and I thought to myself that wherever he is I hope Bix is spinning light.

Maybe I ought not to have taken the notebook. I did break into a house, I picked a window, I stole something. But I am sure Bix would rather I had it to use even a little in my book than let it sit in amongst the GREEN LANTERNs when his stepfather burns them.

I am not a trespasser. I am not a thief either. I am Jerome Foxworthy, and that's it, jack.

3.

The first time I saw Bix was about exactly one year ago. School had just let out, and I was pretty sad as I always am when summer starts. See, I like school. I like fall, I like winter, and spring isn't bad. It never really gets cold in the winter here in Wilmington (North Carolina, there's one in Delaware too) because we are in the South and also we get that Gulf Stream sending in that old warm wind to shore (I have all A's in geography and science too). I do like it when you have to sleep under a weight of blankets and outside you see frost in the shade and everything that has an odor you can smell very clearly, and nothing smells bad.

Most of all, though, I like basketball. In the winter, basketball is the game. Everybody is thinking hoops. Playing hoops too, all over the place—you can get a game anywhere, one on one, three on three half court, five on five full. Indoors, outdoors. Some games split up in the middle and move in or out, if one team shoots better in the breeze. For gym class, you are walking down the hall to get there and from five hundred feet away you can feel it in the bottoms of your feet rumbling through the floors: bammata bammata bammata bam, twenty dudes dribbling those balls on that old gymnasium wood, baby. Nothing anywhere but the main game of basketball mattering the most. That's winter.

But summer changes it all. Summer comes, and people get all easy and slowed and they nod all the time and smile instead of talking fast like they do in winter. But worst of all, once school lets out, all anybody wants to play is baseball. Baseball! Bunch of dudes in knee pants standing up straight and watching each other do very little. Here, Sir, I am throwing this sphere at you. Thank you, Sir, I believe I shall bop it with this stick. Well struck, Sir, and here it comes; I shall endeavor to catch it with my big fat glove that looks like I got a disease. What a tea party.

No tricks. Baseball is like those redcoats in that Revolutionary War (all A's in history too), standing up and pointing their chins, marching in neat lines, loading up those dumb muskets very calm and up front, with polished boots and polished buckles and all kinds of honor . . . and getting their ass kicked by the Swamp Fox. Listen, the Swamp Fox had the idea. He used his brain. Running behind bushes with those bent knees, wearing moccasins and muddy buckskin, dangling his hat on the end of a stick and then popping up to flick a knife out from behind his collar, whisssh! I can tell you one thing: that Swamp Fox, if he lived now, he would be a basketball player. Hoops is for the tricksters. You can bet if there was another war today and it was the dudes who played baseball against the ones who pop the double pump reverse spin lay-ups, the baseballers would never know what hit them.

So I hated baseball, for the game it was, and for how it took hoops right out of everybody's life. I especially didn't like the Little League. It was bad enough when all of my friends would go out to a lumpy old field and pick up sides and whack the ball around. But when adults give them little pretty uniforms and build them little stadiums and put the games on radio and sell soda and candy bars in the stands, then the kids start acting all serious and prissy and like all this attention is the best reason why they ought to play ball. Well, Wilmington is very hip to Little League, or at least to white Little League. There are more than twenty teams. They play doubleheaders four nights a week in these cute little genuine stadiums built just outside town, with lights, scoreboards, announcers, chalk on-deck circles and resin bags, all that crap. Every Friday the paper prints the pictures of four Stars of the Week. On Sunday we get the week's box scores.

The white box scores, that is. The colored league is not nearly as big as the white. Dig, there are probably more left-handed relief pitchers with a missing front tooth and a fork-ball that breaks left to right in the white league than there are players of all kinds in the black. The black people only get four teams together. They play all their games at Catalpa Park. This park has a baseball diamond and big outfield where there isn't a fence but a creek running the border. Anything hit into the creek, even on the bounce, is a home run. It is a nice play to play, with all those huge catalpa trees wearing long bean earrings on their flappy-ear leaves. The spectators sit on the porches of houses across the street that runs along third base line. You only get refreshments if the person who lives there feels like making lemonade and cornmeal cookies.

The games are pretty bad, even for baseball. Those four teams get pretty tired of playing each other over and over all summer long, especially since the talent (if that's what you want to call it) is spread around so even. Listen, two years ago every team finished with the same record, twenty-two wins and twenty-two losses, all tied for first and last place at the same time. They had play-offs and every team went two and two.

Let me ask: Would you like baseball if you were me and this is the highest you could hope to go?

Even so, it was a baseball game where I first saw Bix, one year ago. I didn't want to be there, I didn't want to watch, most of all I sure did not want to start liking some flashy white dude with a face like one of those Vienna choir boy singers that I saw in Raleigh two years ago (I got to say they could sing, though). I did not want to like anything or anybody. But Bix got me, baby.

4.

I was there because my brother Maurice was making his bigtime debut as coach of the Beefy's Lunch team. Maurice is five years older than me. He skipped a grade. This fall he goes off to college up north in Massachusetts, on a scholarship because he's so smart (no smarter than Henri and me on the tests, but just older right now). He wants to be a doctor. Not the same doctor who gives you shots and pills, but one who talks a lot and tries to make you think. He'll probably be pretty good. He practiced enough on Henri and me all these years, though we had plenty from our momma and never felt nearly as bad as he liked to make out. Henri and I agreed long ago to let him practice on us. We thought he was practicing to be a father, not a doctor. We even thought at first he was going to marry Momma and take over, but Momma put us right on that one.

Anyway, Maurice was doing his father-doctor-coach thing with the Beefy's Lunch team last summer, and always coming home from practice with his clipboard and statistics and little stories about how Poke Peters struck out six times but the last two times held his head high which showed positive thinking and Manny Abernathy dropped three fly balls in left field but didn't cry once and wasn't that a step of progress? and so on. Henri, who liked baseball like all the other fools around here, read Maurice's statistic sheet one day and asked Maurice what the initials CA stood for. There was a column underneath them with a space for each boy's name, in between RBI which is runs batted in, and E which is errors. Maurice said CA was Crises Averted. That's Maurice. Momma laughed. She told Henri and me later that the team was coaching Maurice much more than he was coaching them, and it was all right that way.

When the day for the first exhibition game came around, Momma said we had to go and cheer for Beefy's and give our support to old Maurice because he was probably going to fret himself silly. I moaned up a storm because I didn't want to go and watch Manny Abernathy drop fly balls and yet not shed a tear, and Poke Peters whiff but hold his head high, and all of the colored boys averting crises right and left. What a great way to spend a summer evening. But Momma said we had to come. Maurice's team was likely to get creamed and he would need us to cheer for his boys.

The main reason the Beefy's team was set for a creaming was that they were playing the annual exhibition against the white team from the Seven-Up bottling company across town. The Seven-Up team comes every year just before the season and plays one of the black teams at Catalpa Park. Why the Seven-Ups do this nobody knows. No other white team pays any attention to the black league. I used to think it was because the Seven-Ups must be the worst white team and needed to beat up on somebody. I also used to think it must be just because they wanted to primp, in their official uniforms. I still thought so that night, when we went to the game and saw the teams.

I laughed when I saw Maurice's boys down on the field. They looked goofy and proud of it. The team is sponsored by this jolly old fellow named Beefy who owns a lunch counter and tobacco shop in our part of town. The team uniforms are just maroon shirts with gold writing, worn with whatever pants the players' momma didn't care if they tore up. On the front of the shirt is a cartoon of Beefy. Big belly, cigar, eyes all wide and round and smiling like a true fool. On the backs are the numbers, like any team, but not quite. The man who made the shirts used numerals so big he could only fit one digit on the kid-size backs, which is fine if you only have nine players, 1 2 3 4 5 6 7 8 9. But there were fourteen on the team and they all had to have jerseys. So what the man did was, he repeated numbers 1 through 5 but he stuck them on upside down, Ⅰ Ⅰ ⅼ ⅼ ⅼ, so each kid had his own numeral. Man, the ways niggers think to do things sometimes.

The Seven-Ups had no such silliness on themselves. They were decked out in style. Their suits were thick white flannel with green satin piping down the leg and green satin numbers on the back, 1 through 15 with no 13 for bad luck like elevators in tall buildings. Also the Seven-Up slogan was on their backs: above the numbers in green satin it said YOU LIKE IT, and then below the number it said IT LIKES YOU.

They had those baggy pants with elastic at the knee. They had those stockings with no heels or toes, green with three white stripes. They had black leather shoes with pink rubber cleats. And while I watched their pitcher warm up close by the third base line, I saw they even had nice little stitched holes punched in the flannel beneath their arm, so their little nice sweats could dry right away and no unpleasant odors develop.

The best part, to me, was a mostly orange patch sewed over the heart—it was the label off the Seven-Up bottle, this weird thing I had always studied and never figured out. There is a big white 7 and a little UP, which you would expect, though what there is seven of in that drink I will never probably know. But then, off to the side and behind the 7, were these tall, thin silhouettes in dark green of naked people swigging from bottles very gracefully while all these bubbles and streams flowed up around them. I used to look at that label on the bottle whenever I drank a Seven-Up, and I made up all kinds of mysterious half stories about what it all meant but never really got to the magic of it. For a long time I gave up Seven-Up though it was my favorite soda, just because that label bothered me so.

They looked a good deal too fancy. I watched them take infield. They knew what they were doing, but anybody can look good fielding slow rollers hit by a coach whose son is probably the first baseman. Fancy white boys, I thought. Who knows, maybe Maurice's boys will lick them bad?

Then the game started. Maurice's team was up first. Poke spent about three minutes squinting down at Maurice in the third base coach box and finally figured out the signals Maurice was flashing, slapping his head and tapping his right arm and then his left thigh and turning his hat around three times and such as that. What it all meant was, BUNT! Poke laid one down, and beat it out. I'll say this for him, he can fly. The next kid walked. Maurice was busting with pride. He always was saying that it took more brains to take four bad pitches than it did to hit a home run. I always answered that very thing proved baseball was a brainless game, giving more reward for the homer than the walk.

Anyway, the white pitcher didn't look too sharp and I started to think maybe this was Beefy's Lunch's day. The people around me on the porches were whooping it up a bit, with two base runners and nobody out. It didn't even faze them when the next kid struck out, trying to put the ball in the creek, his helmet falling off after every swing. GET IT WET! all the poor fools screamed. DUNK THAT SUCKER, HOO!

The fourth batter was a kid named Oscar who was Maurice's pride and joy, though whether because he was a slugger or just because he was an orphan who hadn't started yet being a knife murderer at ten was not exactly clear. Anyway, Oscar was big, and he looked mean, and he had a swing even I had to say was very pretty. He took two pitches from that white pitcher, and then he lashed one. I mean, the boy LASHED it.

The ball left his bat in a blurry piece of speed you couldn't see for trying. The first you could locate was when it kicked up a spray of dirt just past second base on its way into the outfield and probably clean through the center fielder and all the way into the creek. Every colored there cheered when they saw it, WHOO!

But then out of nowhere the white shortstop whizzed into the picture. He was stretched out full, two feet off the ground, flying like he was shot from a bow and arrow, moving as fast as the ball. WHISH! He snapped his mitt out and snagged that ball ten feet behind second base, and then before he even hit the ground he plucked it out with his bare hand and flipped it backhand to the second baseman, who was standing on the bag. The second baseman went up in a spring over the sliding base runner and whipped a sidearm throw to first that beat Oscar by five feet. BAM BAM BAM a double play and the Seven-Ups trotted in to take their cuts while Poke was still tearing for home not knowing what had happened behind him and the porch fools still rooting, though a bit confused by now.

When we did realize, we clapped again and hooted, but this time it was for those Seven-Ups too. They came to PLAY. And if they wanted to do it in pink rubber cleats, I guess it was okay by me.

5.

The whole game pretty much followed the way the first inning went. The Beefy's boys would smack the ball hard here and there, maybe get on base a few times, and the Seven-Up fielders would nail them. Those white dudes could work the leather. They could work the wood, too. The center fielder hit two balls in the creek on the fly and the shortstop whistled four singles past the pitcher into center field. They won the game about fifteen to two.

I could not take my eyes off that shortstop. He was the only kid I had ever seen who seemed to know with every part of himself just what to do on every single play. His feet were always placed just right to go along with his throwing motion or his gloving, his head was always turned the right way, his steps never left him on the wrong foot when he needed to jump or spin. It was a kind of concentration I had never seen except maybe in Bill Russell once when the Celtics came to Raleigh and played an exhibition basketball game against the Knicks. It was like every cell in the shortstop's body was paying attention, and jumping into the right action along with his mind. Usually it's the mind that kind of leaps ahead and pulls everything else into the act. Not so with this dude.

Another thing was his manners. He could have been the cockiest kid who ever walked. But he was not. He was pleased with the way he played but more than that he looked like he just thought the game was what was really terrific. He never grinned or hooted or anything like that, so I thought he was a little bit of a stiff, but you could see that deep down he was enjoying his whole self, as if he just plain appreciated all the chances baseball gave him. I feel that way with basketball but I never saw it in another kid. So I was interested in this guy.

But I wasn't the only person watching him.

About the second inning this metallic blue car came roaring up the street and screeched to a stop a way down the left field street line. Then this person jumped out and came running up along the line until she was a little bit past third, where she just stopped and kind of took over that spot. There was only a strip of grass maybe

five feet wide between the bag and the
street, and no other spectator even thought
about going in there, because it was practi-
cally part of the field and only players were
on that side of the street. But this woman
didn't seem to notice such things or maybe
to care.

She was about the most beautiful woman
I ever saw. I think my momma is pretty and
stronger-looking than any other person,
but this white woman just knocked you in
the eye like looking at that painting of a
tree hanging over a lake in the state
museum which I always stare at when we
go there and nearly cry for I don't know
what. Her skin was this golden color.
Usually I feel sorry for white people because they don't seem to really have any
color, they look plain and pale and like they
are missing something. But this woman
gave off light right off her face and her
arms and everything that showed. Her hair
was all flashing too. It was somewhere between blond and brown, a color you never
see anywhere, and it was thick and mostly
straight and looked like it was the definition of the word hair out of a dictionary but
better than words could ever be. Most
blacks don't think so much about what hair
is except when they see some like this
woman's. I could see how the people on the
porch around me snatched looks at the

woman's hair moving on her head as she jumped and shook, which she did a lot of. They were amazed like me. It was very pretty to see.

The last thing about her looks was her dress. Not just her dress, but actually everything about the way she was gotten up. She wore this black dress with all kinds of style. It looked as natural on her as an apron on my momma. The way it moved on her made some of the people mutter Oh my land and such things, because it looked so graceful.

But she was weird. She was doing very strange things, and she did them right there in front of everybody as if there wasn't anyone else around. She was jumping up and down and hollering in this loud tight voice, waving her arms and clapping very hard every time something happened around that shortstop. Her voice was the main weird thing. It was all wound up and then let go and it nearly escaped from her every time like a wild bird. She was yelling one strange sound the whole time: BIX BIX BIX.

Yes. That shortstop was Bix. And that woman was obviously his momma.

I felt sorry for him, which made me like him even more. It was like he was more adult than she was, the way she yelled and he just kind of ignored her without being unkindly to her, a couple of times smiling this tight-lip smile very slightly into the air in front of him, for her but not at her, a smile that showed he was aware of her foolishness but also of her admiration and motherly business or whatever it was.

The reason I say whatever it was is that you could see it wasn't just plain old momma's love made her holler. Not just enthusiasm because her boy was making good plays either. There was something else, something she was straining to have or make up for, to Bix and to her too. It was very complicated and I couldn't figure it out clearly but I could see it without doubt. The adults around me on the porch saw it too, and they stopped being entertained by her beauty and her foolishness right fast. After that they looked at her with sort of a pity and a curiosity, and tried not to show any of this to us kids. But I saw it, something unpleasant to see that she couldn't help, like when somebody without an arm takes off his shirt for gym class and you get a look at his stump and it's red and splotchy but of course you can't mind because it's not his fault.

I felt sorry for both of them, even though Seven-Up won.

6.

In the top half of the last inning a big flatbed truck with a metallic green cab rolled up and parked along the third base line. The bed of the truck was sprawled with wooden crates and in the wooden crates were bottles of soft drinks and scattered over the bottles were chunks of ice as big as your hand. It was really very pretty. The bottles were all colors, clear and brown and light green and dark green, and the pop inside was even more colors—red, orange, purple, yellow, green, pink, even blue, which was mint soda and I had never heard of it before. You saw the colors through this chunky blanket of ice that caught the sparkles from the sun which was just getting down there where everything it hits looks better than usual and brighter, and then before you know it it's going to be nighttime. The whole truck was like something out of one of those cartoon movies for kids.

Then another smaller truck with a closed-off back chugged up behind the first. Neither truck moved and nobody came out. They just sat there. You could see the driver of the small truck, a white man with sunglasses, sitting there not watching the last inning, just staring at his hands on the wheel and making a mouth like to whistle, though no one heard any music. The windows of the big truck in front were smoked and you couldn't see who was in there.

They just sat there, up until the very second that the last out was made, a pop-up to shortstop, Bix taking it in very smoothly trotting to his right. Then, right as soon as the ball was in his glove and the game was over, the horn of the big truck cut loose with a blast knocked your hat off, and it had to cut through the blast twice before everybody realized it was playing the first line of TAKE ME OUT TO THE BALL GAME. While it did this the driver of the small truck jumped out very quickly and slung up the sides of the enclosure over the back of his truck, and what do you know, inside was this sort of grill full of must have been a hundred hot dogs and a hundred hamburgers and a crate of rolls and a crate of potato chips (the crinkled kind, I don't like them, but what the heck you can't complain). The man had put on this floppy white marshmallow of a hat like chefs in the funny papers, and he whipped out this huge round board with a thumb hole like an artist uses for his paints only instead of paints it had little pots of relish and chili and mustard and catsup and chow-chow and what-all set into it and he held a brush in his other hand. You'd get yourself a hot dog and hold it up and he would sling things on it with a very large deal of show, I can tell you, but not a drop would he get on your shirt though you would think so.

TAKE ME OUT TO THE BALL GAME blasted that horn TAKE ME OUT TO THE CROWD. And a crowd it was. That horn called people from all across colored-town to come running and the word went back pretty fast that there were free eats. There was plenty. The first few people who finally went up and took some food stuffed all they could hold into their hands and even pockets like they were going to get chased off and wanted to take as much as could be. But more dogs and burgers kept appearing on that grill and you could see there was soda enough forever, so people slowed down and the adults ambled over and the kids ate half of a hot dog and decided they wanted a burger and took two bites and threw it down because now they had to have a chili dog and so on, though not much was wasted I must say. Pretty soon there were all kinds of people there, all ages, eating and talking and running around and sucking down the pop. Some kids stole off empty bottles, to take for deposit, and I know the man in the big truck saw them from way up there, but he did not care and not many did it anyway.

I had myself a burger and an orange and half a grape just because it was there, but didn't finish it because really I don't like soda. A bunch of the younger kids ate up a couple of dogs real fast and then wanted to play ball like the bigger boys had just done, and many black little brothers were pestering their big brothers for their Beefy shirts but not many gave, until some of the Seven-Ups took off THEIR shirts and gave them to a little black kid here and there and then the Beefy's had to do it too. The little boys ran out with the shirts flapping around their knees and hats down over their noses and threw the ball and rolled the bat around and yelled things though they had no idea what they were doing. The white boys that had given up their shirts stood around talking with the black boys who had too, but they kept their arms crossed mostly and I saw they were kind of ashamed for having such pale chests, and I felt sorry for them again.

During all of this I walked over to the side of the big green cab and looked up. It was high, but I could see through the open window and there was a man in there, a white man who wasn't turning gray yet but was almost that age. He was watching everything, looking around taking it all in, and smiling very slightly. Every now and then, when he looked in his rearview and saw the line at the grill getting short, he leaned his hand on the horn and called for more to come and chow. I watched him for quite a while, and then I waited for a quiet time after he blew the horn, and called up. He stuck his head out the window and grinned down at me. He asked if I had enough to eat.

I said yes.

He asked did I have enough to drink.

Yes, I said, I did. And very good, too, I said, though I had to remind myself not to mention the crinkly chips. He looked glad and nodded, and then just hung there. I looked up at him. He said, So, what can I do for you?

I asked him if he was the owner of the Seven-Up plant. He said he certainly was.

I asked him if he was having a good time.

Oh yes, he said, and hit the horn. It hurt your ears when you were so close to the truck, and I had to clap my hands over mine. He apologized.

Why do you do it? I said. Why do you put on this big deal?

He looked down at me for a second or two, smiling that slight little smile, and then he stuck his arm out and patted the slogan painted on the side of the truck. I stepped back and read: YOU LIKE IT, IT LIKES YOU.

That's the secret of life, he said.

Or at least the secret of a good cookout, I said. He laughed and said maybe my way of saying it was better, and then he leaned on the horn for so long laughing that I had to hold my ears and get away from the truck but I really did not mind much.

7.

Sometime in the middle of all the excitement I remembered that shortstop Bix. I was not sure whether I wanted to talk to him or just kind of check him out when he wasn't playing ball, but I was curious to see him for sure.

I looked around down in the crowd, but there was too much crowd to see clearly about. I made my way back and climbed up on the porch where I had watched the game from. Nobody was there now but this old granny I had not seen before but everybody had left alone in a rocker in one corner. She paid me no mind, she was busy shaking her head and babbling about all the colors of the soft drinks shining in those bottles out on the flatbed. Red brown green orange yellow, she kept saying, red orange brown yellow green.

I stood and looked around for the Bix boy. I kept an eye peeled for his mom too. She would be easier to spot, and I wouldn't have minded another sight of her anyway.

I have a way I use in crowds sometimes when you are looking for somebody, you let your eyes pick lines and make a square containing a small part of the crowd and you check it out. Then you move on to the next square and take your peeks. Well, I shot through the crowd twice and saw no sign of that Bix and his black-dress momma.

He was gone. They were gone together. They did not stick around for dogs and burgers and lemon-lime and colored folk.

All of a sudden, I got mad all out of shape, furious. Here one minute I had my gumption up and was just about ready to go talk to a white stranger and ask maybe to learn a few things about baseball—baseball! I hated baseball!—which was a big deal for me. I had worked myself up pretty much, I guess. And then all of a sudden I was left there, and I got angry as a wasp. Everything that had been going in a nice direction inside me turned backward all nervous and meanish, and next thing you know I was grinding my teeth and thinking up ugly things. Pretty little white boy! Had to leave after the game and couldn't stay and eat a crude old burger and make buds with the team he beat. Probably was nice and safe at home right this minute being served a steak and green beans cut slanty-wise by some quiet old colored in a white jacket.

That momma would be fondling her pearls with one hand and reaching over once every minute to stroke the boy's lovely hair off his forehead but he wouldn't even look at her, just keep slicing his beef with a silver knife though all she wanted was a little notice. Well, that cracker was going to be no friend of mine! I said to myself and felt all righteous, though lord knows why.

Man, it was so strange the way I latched onto this sudden hate like hate was precious and not by no means to be let go of. I stood there beside that foolish old granny, listening to her go through those colors Orange green my oh my red and brown, and never thought to wonder how foolish I was being coming up so sudden with such ugliness. I just ground my teeth and looked out to the field where that shortstop had made me almost even dig baseball, and smirked. The hamburger felt pretty hard in my stomach.

In the third square of the crowd I saw my momma and Maurice and the white coach, Mo no doubt going over some fine points of how to avert a crisis with the bases full and a left-handed curveball pitcher on the mound with an orphan at the plate high on airplane glue thinking he is supposed to run to third after he hits the ball and does so. My momma looked bored, and started to look around like she hoped she could find somebody and I knew it was me she was looking for to come save her from Maurice's chatter. But I did not come. I was too mad. I snuck off the porch over the railing behind the granny and lit off for home all by myself.

I was just about home when I heard TAKE ME OUT TO THE BALL GAME TAKE ME OUT TO THE CROWD blaring up through the sky and a couple of little punks come hooting out of their house and start to run to where the song was.

Shut up you old white fool, I yelled. The kids stopped and looked at me and I glared and they scooted back inside and did not come out. Too bad.

SECOND PART

8.

You cut through the backyards first, all of them no problem except Mrs. Stokes who worries about her tomatoes and thinks every boy in town lies awake plotting how to steal them. You get to hop three fences. Then you come to town but you don't go in, cutting instead down Left Alley which even though it is dark is no trouble, because all the store owners keep their back doors open and could hear if anybody jumped you. At the end of the alley you have to pop over a high fence and if you are wearing a stretchy shirt or too big for you like one of Maurice's sweat shirts from the high school track team, then you can stick the ball up under while you jump.

You cut across Marsh Fields then and pretty soon you stop seeing streets and only trees are there, growing out of the mucky ground. You stop seeing people too, especially in the summer on account of the bugs.

So you head right into the forest, or maybe it is just woods, even though there does not seem to be a path. You know where to go. And pretty soon, just when you think the woods are going to get even darker and moister and cooler, you step right out into the clearing and see it.

The prettiest little concrete half-court basketball place in town.

The trees are high enough to cut the sun out and the shade keeps it cool enough that most of the bugs shy off. Still, it is bright in there, kind of a greenish blue light, looking just like the way hemlocks smell. The only sound you hear, except for the squeak of your Chucks and the bammata of the ball and the pong of the steel backboard and the ching of the nets, is whistles from birds in the forest. There is one old hawk who sits on a red pine branch on the edge of the clearing and watches sometimes, but he never makes any noise. Mostly it is smaller birds inside. One time the hawk got himself a squirrel that came out to see what was making the bammata. I suppose he waits in case another one is stupid enough to try it again.

You can have this court anytime by yourself. Nobody knows it is there. Nobody is interested in playing basketball in the summer, anyway. You have to wonder whose idea it was to build a basketball court out in the middle of the forest behind Marsh Fields. It may not seem like a good idea because the court is not crowded, but when you play there, smelling those hemlocks as you spin through the cool air and popping those jumpers facing any direction without sun in your eyes, and always finding it all to your own game, then you think it is a very great idea indeed. You think this court was built by somebody who loved the game you love, and you think he was a genius, like you.

You can play in the winter too. The trees are still green and the air is not too cold. The hawk is gone in the winter, but you don't miss him much.

9.

That court in the woods was where I spent last summer. Every day after breakfast I cut on out there, taking a canteen full of Hi C and my ball and sometimes a banana sandwich or something though mostly it was too hot to eat. I played all morning until it got about to noon, the only time the sun got bad in my court. Then I would lie down in the pine shade and sip a little C and maybe stack a z or two. I would wake up feeling cool and crisp and full of speed, so I hit the court again until evening time.

I was always by myself. Well, almost always, and the one time I was not was enough to make sure I never brought anybody along ever again. I did not want to bring anybody even then, but I ran into Poke Peters in Left Alley, sitting out behind his father's grocery, drinking a Dr. Pepper with M&Ms in it and singing In the jungle the mighty jungle the lion screws tonight. That song happened to be about my favorite last summer and I thought Poke was stupid and nasty to mess it into some silly dirtiness, and I told him so.

He ignored me and squinted underneath his baseball cap which was a fake Durham Bulls, with the front D peeling off. Play some catch with me, he said.

No, I said, and made to move off.

Okay, play some roll-a-bat.

Forget it, I said. Roll-a-bat is the dumbest thing anybody ever thought of to kill time, and although I did not tell Poke, I would rather have run a mile in last year's sneaks than do it. What it is, you hit the ball as hard as you can to a person out in the field and he catches it and from where he stands he slings the ball along the ground and tries to bop the bat, which you have laid on the ground where you hit from. If he hits it he gets to bat and you got to go catch and roll. Typical sort of jive for a baseball lover to think up.

Poke took a pull at his drink, getting all the M&Ms, but then he sort of thought of me and politely spit a few back in and offered me a swig. I shook my head. He said, Where you headed, then?

I was carrying a basketball so it was a pretty stupid question, but I also could not say I was going swimming or anything like that, though I would have because everybody knows Poke hates to swim or even bathe.

Going to shoot around some, I said.

Poke polished off the Dr. Pepper with a slurp, threw the bottle straight up over his head and smiled at me right in the eyes while it crashed on the roof.

James Knox Polk Peters Jr. you get your young black butt in here right now where I can beat it blue! screamed Poke's daddy's voice from back inside the store. Poke kept smiling but hopped off the crate and said, Let's us go do some hoop.

Now, only somebody who doesn't know anything will call hoops hoop without the s on the end. It is just like when you meet someone from the North and they want to pretend to talk southern as a joke and they say you-all to only one person. No southerner ever said you-all to only just one person, it being the very word to use for more than one, obviously. Don't ask me why hoops is hoops and not hoop, but it is. Poke and other baseball people are liable to this mistake. It shows how little they know.

But Poke was determined to come and play. My manners are too good to tell somebody being friendly that they are about as welcome as the whooping cough, so I let him tag. All the while we walked I was afraid he was going to like my court so much he would come back and bring his jive friends, but this was not so. He got bored with walking real soon, and did not pay attention well enough to remember how to get there. Also he kept moaning about the bugs and about how I must be crazy and hate people to go so far out of town to do a little hoop. When we got to the woods he even stopped and looked at me with one eye closed and a suspicious frown.

You trying to trick me, nigger?

No, Poke, I said. But if you don't want to come . . .

You trying to get me to come swimming in some nasty creek in these woods?

No creek in these woods, I said, wishing there was one and we had to swim across it two miles underwater.

He cocked his head up, still one eye closed, and sniffed the air. No, he said, I believe you telling the truth. I can smell swimming water if it's nearabouts, and I don't smell a thing now. He sniffed again, and I think he inhaled a mosquito for he fell to coughing and whining something awful. Finally we got through the woods and out to the court.

What happened for the rest of the morning was too awful to tell all of. First, Poke wanted to stand me one on one, but I scored six straight buckets and ran him so bad he started hacking and drooling and moaning until he had to sit in the shade

and smoke a cigarette, which stank everything up and made ME start to hack. Then
he came back and insisted that we play
HORSE. I hit three jumpers and he
missed but then I missed a left-handed
lay-up and he took the ball and stood behind the backboard with his back to it,
and while I watched amazed and scornful,
for who would ever use such a shot, he
bounced the ball backwards between his
legs and it bounced off the pole, hit the
back of his head which he held rigid,
sailed up over the board and dropped
through the net.

Make it, sucker, he said.

That is not a shot, I said. Only a fool
would call that a shot.

Make it, he said.

I bounced it off my foot off to the edge of
the woods.

Eat yourself an H, baby, said Poke.

Then he lay down on the foul line with his
head pointed toward the basket, on his
back with his feet in the air. He tossed the
ball onto his feet and snapped his ankles
up, rolling the ball off his toes into the air
about a foot and a half. While it was in the
air he tucked his legs back and when it
came down he snapped them back and
kicked the ball backwards over his head. It
hit the board so hard the whole pole shook,
but the ball shot through the net.

Do it to it, he said. Let's see how much hoop class you got.

That kind of thing doesn't measure basketball ability, I started to say, but he shook his head and said Poo poo poo, nigger. Make it go, or you got O.

I didn't even toss the ball up onto my feet right, and that was it.

He missed his next one, some shot off his rear end while doing the shingaling to the song Do You Love Me, which he sang in a high voice. I hit two jumpers and closed out the game, and we left, but I was shaking. Poke was happy, singing and giving me grief about his shots I didn't make and ripping pine needles off trees to suck on and picking up pine cones to whip at trees with a windup he thought looked like Mudcat Grant's. I was not happy. I felt like I had wasted a day, wasted more than that too—wasted my whole private thing. Being alone in a place is one of those things you can only have for one long spell, and when you break it you are never the same quite again, you cannot get it back exactly right.

But Poke never troubled me again to come back, and he forgot all about my court I am sure, and I never let myself get anywhere near anybody on my way to play that summer again. After a couple of weeks, I did have my private thing back, and it felt exactly right, though I later found it wasn't, though I do not think Poke's intruding had anything to do with the weirdness I grew.

10.

My momma was the first person to notice, and the only person to notice, except for me, which I did after she tuned me in on it. I had no idea I was doing anything funny. Every day I slipped off with my ball and every evening I came home, and in between, there were my moves. Moves were all I cared about last summer. I got them down, and I liked not just the fun of doing them, but having them too, like a little definition of Jerome. Reverse spin, triple pump, reverse dribble, stutter step with twist to the left, stutter into jumper, blind pass. These are me. The moves make the man, the moves make me, I thought, until Momma noticed they were making me something else.

One nice thing about my momma is, she never gets on you for what you are not doing. I mean, she never looks away from the things you do only to notice what isn't on the plan. This is the most important thing in getting along with your son, or getting along with anybody, and I can tell you because I copy it from her and it makes good sense. You don't go looking at the things people don't do, when they already be doing plenty in other areas. If your son collects stamps, why you want to go fussing at him because he doesn't play the clarinet? Check out his stamps, man.

Maurice used to nail me for all kinds of things I did not do, complaining that I was going to get unrounded and all off balance unless I developed this or that side of myself and stopped being content. He picked things up from his studies, books that said the normal kid was supposed to play at least three sports a year with equal enthusiasm, split his love equally between two parents, like science as much as English and music as much as gym, have white friends and Negro friends and Chinese friends and all kinds of people we probably don't even have in Wilmington anyway. I was wrong on all counts according to Mo, but most of the counts I couldn't help. For example, my father got killed when I was hardly even born, hit by a truck and knocked into many pieces according to my cousin Terry who is eight years older than me and saw things. Now, I couldn't go loving him, could I, when I never heard a word from the dude? My momma was too much to count as just one parent, anyway, and nobody could go off balance loving her. I had to keep quick and keen to keep up with loving all the things she was. Maurice would have said so too, if he thought about it that way.

As for liking all subjects the same, I only knew one person who did that and he was this kid named Hutchins who got nothing but C's right down the line, smiling all the while and doing his homework half right and half wrong no matter what the class. What a goof. He reminded me of the black Little League, every team the same record, same number of wins and losses, all tied up. Look, every kid I know likes some things better, some going for chocolate milk which makes me throw up personally, some going for Seven-Up, and me liking nothing as much as cold blue water. Every kid has his favorite drink, his favorite subject, most even have his favorite parent.

So Maurice made noise and tried to get me to play with his old chemistry set instead of reading, with its old caked-up flasks and cracked test tubes so you'd be lucky not to explode yourself, and things like that. My momma finally told him to leave me be. She knew I was all right and not about to get into any bad ways, all on my own. Some kids you can trust, and that's me.

Even so, last summer my momma even asked me a couple of times if I was playing with anybody or if I was okay. I was doing the solo hoops thing a little more than ever. She also said I was starting to talk to myself even when other people were there. This shook me up a little bit. I asked what she heard me say. She said she could never tell, sounded like code. So next time I was out shooting I suddenly tuned in, and sure enough I was just chattering away, a twist above a whisper, and what I was saying was, what my imaginary opponent in one on one was seeing—all my moves like a catalogue. I was naming them off and telling him what they were doing to him, you know: Here I go baby reverse spin up for double pump off the glass you got them legs crossed and eyes too SWISH! Stuff like that, for almost every shot.

Whew! I never used to talk to myself like that. Oh, once in a while I would imagine a game, but never one on one, always big team things under the lights in Boston Garden, like any kid. I hear the baseball dudes pretending they are batting against Whitey Ford all the time. But I only did this once a week or so. Rest of the time, I was always just concentrating on my moves, how every part of me felt when I left the ground or let it fly or came down too early off a spin. I never needed to pretend

anything. I never needed to imagine I was
going against somebody. I never needed
anything but my own self making my own
game, and it didn't feel selfish or anything
stupid and lonely, because I was not
retreating or being shy. I was just playing
and concentrating on the thing right there,
right then. So how come all of a sudden I
am dreaming up some bad dude to beat?

The next thing to look at was the funny
feeling I had, that my mystery opponent
was not just any old mystery opponent. I
had a little twiggle inside that told me I
knew him. Maybe not just as he was on that
court in my head, but that I had made him
out of somebody. So I just kept on playing
with him, but watching now, trying to let
myself go on with this weird jive but keeping an eye on what I might let slip. (This
watching and being natural is a pain, and I
will never do it again, I can tell you.) Sure
enough, though, one day I flashed a
behind-the-back dribble at my enemy and
slipped by to the inside and rolled it off my
left hand on the reverse and it was just so
humiliating and nasty that I was screaming inside and the screams were all for his
shame and helplessness and they were so
pointed at him that I could not miss him
there:

You guessed it. My opponent in my head
was that white shortstop.

Man! What a foolish thing! I just stood there, the ball bouncing itself out after coming through the cords, and I thought, What kind of weirdo have I become? Here I am playing for the hate of somebody I don't know and saw once and when I saw him all he was was beautiful, and I don't even notice when I have built him up for something and tear him down every day instead of playing sharp and simple. I am not usually a kid who slips into bad habits. I know what I am doing every step—that's why I do it, because I am sure it is good. So for this thing to sneak up on me . . .

I cut out this mystery enemy business for the next two weeks, the last two of the summer. No white shortstop Bix boy secret ghost loser taking all my fakes and giving me the left side. I kept an eye on myself and there was not a single word of whispered jive.

But you know what? I had no fun. And worse, during those two weeks, I didn't have my moves, not even the moves I had built up over all those years before I had to lay them on a ghost.

I was pretty worried. But then this thing with the school started, and took my mind right off the problem. At least for a while.

11.

A week before school started, my momma got a letter from the superintendent of the schools. What it said was, Chestnut Street Junior High School was about to get itself integrated by one colored child, name of Jerome Foxworthy.

Chestnut is the biggest white school in Wilmington. It had nine hundred white students, grades four through eight. Now it was going to add one black sucker. Man, what a ratio.

What happened is this: The Congress passed a law said schools had to integrate. Not everybody was happy about this, black as well as white. We had good schools to ourselves and you knew where you stood all day. But since it was always made a thing of that the crackers were the ones doing the keeping out, then it was made a thing of that they had to start letting jigaboo boys and girls into their schools. Nobody ever thought to make the jigaboos let little crackers into their schools. Always it was them that did the keeping out and letting in.

Okay, so when the rules were clear, the school board had to get some black kids fast. Otherwise, I don't know what. Maybe they throw the superintendent in jail in Washington DC or something. Ha ha. So the school board gets very clever when it comes to that fine place, Chestnut. What they did was, they expanded the Chestnut district, adding one full square block of niggertown. All kids in that new block had to come to the big Nut. Guess whose house was the only one with any kids on that block, and guess who was the only junior-high-age kid in that house? You got it: baby Jerome.

And the school board knew it too, don't go fooling yourself.

Now, I didn't like the idea much. Not so much because I was going to be Mister One Constitutional Negro among all the palefaces, but just because I was going to miss going to Parker, the big black junior high. Parker was as good as Chestnut and probably better, and I already knew three of the teachers there on account of having taken advanced classes during fifth and sixth grade which nobody at the grade school could teach me. I knew Mr. Beans, the math man, and Miss Tipper, the

English lady, and Mr. Wayburn, who took care of the science at Parker. I did well in all of these classes and I liked the teachers fine. They like me too, and they had all these special deals lined up for me when I got there, this time with a few other smartypantses so I wouldn't be by myself accelerating anymore. That would be nice. Ever since I took these smarts tests in third grade, I had about two classes a year taught to me and me alone while all the other kids got to hang together.

Worse than missing these three teachers, I would miss Coach Newcombe, who already knew me and was watching out for me to give his junior varsity basketball team a break by starting at guard. Listen, I'm not just bragging. The man saw me playing one day driving by in his car when I was in a three on three with bigger boys on the Parker tar courts, and I was dishing off the passes and popping the ten-footer and looking dandy. He waited for me and drove me around and home, talking all the while and encouraging me to keep practicing up to the day I came to Parker and could step onto the team. He even gave me a ball, saying it was a school ball but I think he bought it himself, for me to practice with and a pump and needle too, so I would get used to the official bounce. It was the only ball I used for the past two years.

Man, I was torn up at the thought of missing my chance to make good for Coach Newk. Henri had been a flop of a forward for him, all leg and no eye or hustle, and I wanted to get the Foxworthy thing straightened out but true. Plus I had gotten used to seeing myself putting on that Parker purple jersey and trunks, and I even had my number picked out, which was going to be 10 if I could.

There were my friends too. You may have seen smarty kids who walked around all day hugging big books and squinting and never getting along with anybody else, but that's not my boy Jerome. I may not like baseball but I like my buddies, even though I don't see as much of them as most other dudes do of theirs. I did not have one best bud, you know, somebody you sleep at their house as easy as at your own, somebody you trade swigs with on each and every drink without wiping on your sleeve, which I wouldn't do anyway because the sleeve is probably dirty as sin, somebody you just plain love to look at and be around. Funny, but I never had a best bud like that. Maybe it is because I couldn't quite cut the time into my life on account of all the running to classes and slipping off to my hoops. Maybe I had time enough to devote to making good friends but not to making a best. It never bothered me, because I figured I just hadn't met the right dude. You know, some kids, they feel like they have to have a best buddy even if there is nobody around they like that much. They just take whoever they think comes closest and that seems like the wrong way to me. I have my pals Timothy, Markham, Pinky, Joseph, Alton, Booger, Tin Can, Henry, Perry and Thomas. There are more besides. Plus I have my momma, and Henri and Maurice. I don't lack anything.

But I knew if I went to Chestnut I was suddenly going to lack Timothy, Markham, Pinky, Joseph and the rest of those boys. They would fall along with Mr. Beans and Miss Tipper and Mr. Wayburn and Coach Newk. Were there white people as good at Chestnut to take their place?

During this time when it was revealed about me going to the new school, my momma could have really blown it. She was pretty mad at the cheapo way the school board was trying to obey the integration law, and she did not hide this. She said it was a disgrace and a mockery of the spirit of the equality the law was trying to put over, and such as that. I remember it all pretty well, because when my momma talks to me she says things very clearly and I always like that she speaks like I am an adult. What brains I didn't get from

Momma I grew on account of her treating me like I had them.

Anyway, she spoke like this for a couple of days and made a few phone calls. Then she sat down, still angry in a collected sort of way, and she explained to me that I must not think she was mad just because she thought I was going to be in trouble. She said her mad was a principle mad. She said it looked like I was in fact going to go to Chestnut and that was going to be just fine. I should not let her agitate me into a lack of confidence. Okay?

Okay, I said. Listen, I felt all right about it, in spite of knowing I was going to miss everybody. I am not cocky, but I know who I am and that I will be fine anywhere. My momma said she thought so too, and most kids would have whipped up all this special caution and determination but she knew I would just be Jerome same as I always was and that was the only way to go anywhere. She said when a person acts unnatural they are doomed to be unhappy. You never trick anyone but yourself when you try, she said. I told her all my tricks went down on the basketball court. We shook hands and I ate lunch, hot turkey sandwich.

After that we didn't talk anymore about the big deal, we just went about preparing for school like every September. My momma made no more angry calls, which was okay with me either way. I got through with explaining everything to the kids I knew, and that was okay too. A few of them called me Crackerjack, which means somebody who likes white people better and moons around them, but they were mostly kidding and if they weren't, too bad for them.

We went out shopping and bought some new corduroys and shirts and a new pair of high black Chucks for dress. I like the corduroys that have flecks of all kinds of colors in them and feel like rugs when they are washed. I also like plain light blue shirts with the kind of collar you can wear a tie under, only I never wear ties, so Momma bought three of those. She also got me a new lunch box, one with Crusader Rabbit on it, the only cartoon I still liked and am not ashamed to say so. There's all kind of mystery in Crusader and I like things you have to think about. I never watch any other TV. We don't have one on account of my momma thinks they are trash mostly, but she lets me go to Beefy's on Saturdays for his Kids Breakfast, when he gives us pancakes and coffee milk and one fried egg for fifteen cents and lets us sit at the counter and watch cartoons for an hour every week.

About three days before school I had a visitor. It was Mr. Terrence, the principal of

Parker! Man, I couldn't believe he came all the way to see me. He was famous for being a tough dude, but he seemed okay to me, very sharp and businesslike which most kids think is meanness but is really just the way adults act when they want to treat you like you were more than some baby.

Mr. Terrence came just to tell me about how I would find things to be at Chestnut. He brought along all these charts and graphs and test score results citywide and so on. We talked for almost an hour and my momma made him coffee and cookies. What he showed me was that the white schools were a little faster in English and a little slower in Math and they offered more subjects. He went over every subject I had taken and showed me where I would likely fit in at the Nut. He told me about their accelerated programs, and said he had recommended that I not be put into them until my second semester there, so I could taste the regular routine first and not jump into things as both a new racial item and a new intellect item too. He used words like that, which is fine with me, I know lots of words.

Then he showed me these test scores, first on graphs and then actual people's scores. What it boiled down to is that I was the second highest kid in the whole city for those going into seventh grade, so I didn't have to hold myself low or back on any account. I told him it was nice of him to tell me but I didn't need any test to tell me that. My mother smiled and told him I was not brash but just happy, and he said bravo, especially since the only kid who scored above me was a white girl who spent at least one month a year with a mental doctor because she couldn't keep up with her brain and got all messed up.

I asked if she went to Chestnut. He said yes, she was the star pupil. I said, maybe not for long. He laughed and handed me a cookie, which I ate of course.

12.

Chestnut and all those white people turned out to be no big deal right away. I used to sort of have this backheaded idea that there weren't as many types of white people as there were types of black people—you know, they were all more alike than we are—but I was wrong. The Nut was like a city, and it had its rich and poor and jocks and brains and pretties and uglies and mopes and clowns, all thrown together like anyplace else. On the whole I say white kids are more nervous than black kids but otherwise they have the same sort of different kinds of people.

I guess my situation was ripe for trouble, being the only coon in the forest, like one of my uncles said. But nobody made any more trouble than usual for me. One kid named Turk, although he was blond and in Turkey they have dark hair, got me into a fight on my first day. He stood in front of me and started to let fly with some nasty names and such, but I cut him off and said Look, you want to fight, so okay let's get down to it, and I poked him on the chin and he looked startled and so I jabbed him in the eye to get him more used to the idea and then I dove on him. He sort of squirmed and wouldn't wrestle me, I guess because he hated touching a nigger which was fine because I had an easy time without him resisting. I rolled him over, sat on his chest, smacked him in the face a couple of times and said, If you want to duke, duke, if you want to call names, call names. He shut up and nobody bothered me again for more than a few Nigger! calls. Just as well for them. I can throw the hands, baby. I don't like to, but I can. You always get in a fight now and then when you are new to a place, whether it's blacks fighting you or whites or whatever. It's not a racial thing always, that's just an excuse. Guys like Turk would probably fight in the dark when they couldn't see what kind of people you are.

My classes got along okay. I was ahead in three, Science and Math and Health, but there was a little new stuff in the new books and I could pretend I was just sticking even. In English, Chestnut had the edge, mostly from making us do all kinds of reading on our own and a book report every week, and you couldn't jive Miss Burno either, swapping books and swapping reports and doing what I did a few times in a pinch in sixth grade, which was, I made up a book altogether for the report and wrote on it, summarizing the plot that was not there and naming names that were not named. This was almost more fun than if I had read a real one. But I knew right away Miss Burno would catch me. She had eyes like mercury out of a broken thermometer, man they could move and take it all in.

I liked the reading she made us do, but I did not like the crap she picked to read out loud in class. It was this magic-kingdom kiddie jive, with a hero the same age as us, supposed to suck us in and make us feel like, Hey, that could be little old me in that magic kingdom, whoopee-doo! instead of knowing we were just listening to an old spinster read a book in North Carolina on an afternoon in a room with the heat turned up too blame high. It's dishonest when people try that one on kids. Mostly, though, magic-kingdom stories are all the same thing, with a few new animals or spells shoved in to make it different from the ones that came before, but not too different. And did you ever notice how these writers think up a weird problem that just gets you interested, some magician against a mad king with a dragon all balanced off in this system of things that might happen at the same time, or something, but instead

of working it out, just when you get interested to see how the guy is going to pull it
off, well, then there is some big sudden
catastrophe or invention that bails the good
guy out without the writer having to think
up anything clever? And Suddenly There
Was a Flood, or some crap like that, and all
the baddies washed away to Bad Person
Island out to sea. Bye-bye, baddies, see you
in the next book, baby, only you be wearing
a new hat.

I had two new classes I never had before
too. They taught me as much about white
people as they did about the actual subjects.

First was French. The French language.
Je m'appelle Jerome, man, and je suis un
étudiant de français and a good one. The
first day, the lady in counseling asked if I
wanted Spanish, French, or German. Hey, I
thought she was talking about what kind of
salad dressing for lunch. Languages? I had
never heard about learning languages.
Nobody ever mentioned they taught them
at Parker, and my brothers never took
them even at high school. Niggers speaking
German? Come on! I asked the lady what I
was supposed to take the language for. She
said, for your foreign language require-
ment, of course. Right. Give me some of
that French, my lady, and let me get down
to requiring.

French! I was amazed. The French language. I was going to be speaking the same words those dudes and damsels chattered over there where it's night while it's day in Wilmington, Caroline du Nord. It hit me that I could go over there and talk to them one day if I was a good boy and did my lessons. It was the first time I ever really caught a look at how something from school might work outside in the world. Suddenly I thought the dude who thought to teach it in seventh grade was a genius, a lot smarter than the dude who made us learn algebra and such. What good did it do me to learn quadratic equations? Why, it got me through my math quiz, that's what. What about learning North Carolina history, which I had three grades? Well, that was so I could pass those tests asking where Cornwallis landed and such crucial things as who invented the double-sided spinning jenny on account of he was from Beaufort.

I took right to the idea of French class, and I took right to the lingo itself too. The teacher was this white woman named Madame Dupont, but she wasn't French though it was a French name. After three days, which we learned how to pronounce a few basic things and the pronouns and the rules for verbs, after that we were allowed only to speak French in that class! Anybody talked English, they got themselves ignored. Right there in a school and you could not talk English! Man, that room was something special to me, a little world by itself. When I walked in I felt completely new. I never realized before then how much my way of talking was what made me who I thought and other people thought I was. Take away your habits with the words, and check out who is left, and you see that a lot of things can be fixed if you let them go with the lingo. Now, I didn't have a lot of bad things to be let go, but I did like the idea of being able to start from scratch and build myself a personality step by step through the words I talked, knowing every step what I was doing, which you do not know when you learn English starting at one year old and picking up all kinds of trash in yourself.

French was great. There were all kinds of rules, but in between the rules there were all sorts of little spots where you could make a choice and make your own way, places where nobody else would react like you do. I saw it. Most of the kids in the class were smarties, must have been because it was a small class, half the size of normal, and everybody clicked right into French and kept the pace speeding along. Usually in any class you get some duds. No duds in French, though. Those white kids were something else. I had been in accelerated black classes but the black kids always knew they were out ahead and acted it. These white kids learned like they didn't pay attention but picked it up like eating breakfast. They came to school every day just KNOWING they were going to get it. The word that kept coming to me was, PRECISE. They were precise from when they took off their coats, but they didn't even try, many of them sloppy in dress or the way they talked at least in English. Listen, when blacks learned they KNEW they were learning.

That was the class that gave me hints of what some of the best things about white people were. The class that showed me some of the worst things was one called Communications.

Communications was a class full of nothing but useless trash. The teacher was this flashy dude named Egglestobbs. He was about twenty-five, with wavy brown hair and big old blue eyes flirting around under his low eyelids. The girls giggled when he looked away after glancing at them. What kind of charge he got out of them, I don't know. He was ridiculous to me. He always made big gestures when he was talking, paying as much attention to his hands as his words and sometimes even stopping in the middle of a sentence to watch his fingers flutter or his arm wave, forgetting he was talking and just digging his appendages. Other times it would be the opposite. He would look at you and fix on you and then after a second he would say something like Well, do you agree? even though he never said anything to agree with. If you said you had no idea, he would laugh and say you were not hip to body language and the girls would sigh and giggle at you and at the word body.

You see, body language was this guy's big deal. He was an official body language professor, with an official degree in it and all like that. Where they give such a thing I can't imagine, but I never want to go to such a school. It is like getting a degree in water sculpture or writing with air.

Egglestobbs said people all communicated much deeper and more sincerely without the words but by what they did besides. The way you hung your leg over the chair didn't mean anything about trying to be comfy, what it meant was I hate your guts if it was at one angle or let me kiss you on the lips if it was another angle. The shake you gave to your hand when you make a point in arguing is not just to show you're excited about being right, but it is a precise expression of hostility or envy or friendly disagreement depending on which way you shake and how much. Man, we spent two whole days shaking our pointed finger and writing down ninety different ways the shook finger said things. Did you wiggle or did you tremble? Aha, there's a difference. Is your back straight or crooked? Better check because it says too different things. Do your toes go in or out? Is your hair combed wet or dry? How many ways can you wrinkle your beezer? Do you show your teeth when you say the letter s? All very critical stuff.

It was not so bad just hearing this junk. I mean, I could tell it was eyewash and I just goofed on how silly Egglestobbs and his girls were. The bad thing was, it caused everybody around to start getting very worried about what they were saying when they didn't know what their ear or ankle was doing, and then why they were saying it and whether anyone was getting it and so on. You'd be talking to somebody and all of a sudden he would stop and check out his hands and feet and ask Is my back straight? Well, what the heck did it matter? Everybody stopped talking natural for a while. And they stopped listening natural, too. You would be chatting away telling something and someone would be nodding at you and then say some weird response. You'd say What are you talking about and they'd tell you they were replying to your body language. Something you said with your eyelid or angle of the torso. What a pile of doody.

As I said, this was the worst case of white man's genius I saw. Make something out of nothing and turn everybody very nervous. It was only one class, though. Still, I didn't like to think about what other foolishness they might get behind.

13.

You probably wonder why the first thing I did wasn't check out the basketball tryouts. Well, I knew that at Parker hoops tryouts did not start until football season was over, which is to say about late November. But then one day after school, when I had stayed after with Madame Dupont in French to get my reflexive verb action down just right, I was walking to my locker and I felt it in the soles of my feet: bammata bammata bammata. Somewhere down that hallway, someone was dribbling basketballs.

Naturally I wanted to go check it out. It is in your body when you love ball. Your hands start to curve and spread, your wrists feel like oiled metal, your feet want to kick up off the ground and you just know you are light and trim and can get up in that sky and stay there. Man, I love it and I was very excited all of a sudden that day.

Lucky, I had worn my high blacks to school instead of my loafers, which I usually do until it's too cold out for canvas which lets the wind whistle through. I had on a pretty old pair of corduroys, getting a little snug, but floppy down at the feet which was bad, and a sweater with a T-shirt underneath. Usually I hate T-shirts and do not wear them under shirts, but with sweaters you got to have something to keep the wool off your skin. Very quickly I thought out what I could do to get in playing shape with my clothes, and then I went quietly down to the place where the dribbling came from and saw, sure enough, that it was the gym. There were two double doors. There was something else too:

Thumbtacked up on the left-hand door was a manila folder opened up and written in crayon BOYS' BASKETBALL TRYOUTS WEDNESDAY THURSDAY. This was Wednesday. I was right on time, baby.

Very fast now, because I heard somebody blow a whistle inside, I ran back to my locker, shucked off my sweater, tightened my laces, and ran into the first classroom I could find.

Sitting behind the desk was old Egglestobbs.

He looked up at me, and smiled one of those smiles that people give you when they think they know just exactly what kind of foolishness you are up to, and you don't know it is foolish yet, being dumber than they.

Scissors, I said. He pretended not to hear me, and leaned back and put his fingertips together under his chin and pooched out his lips, which I guess was his way of studying someone, but to me looked like a pretty weird bunch of body signals.

High excitement, he said, as if he were talking to some great scientist standing beside him. Haste. A great hastiness—notice the angle of the torso.

Notice the fact that I ran in here panting, I said. Any scissors in that desk, Mr. E.?

The spread of the feet is revealing too, he said, nodding slowly and dropping his eyebrows. They enclose an acute, rather than an obtuse, fan of degrees. This of course denotes physical anxiety and not a little emotional disconfidence. He raised his brows and put on this fakey smile which I knew meant he was going to include me in the conversation now. Feeling a little inadequate, are we? Though probably, he said back to his ghost scientist, primarily in a physical sense.

Feeling very late for basketball tryouts, I said, trying not to get sassy, completely in a physical sense. Also feeling the need for a pair of big fat school scissors which I bet you got in that desk drawer if you would just let me check.

I went over and pulled open the drawer, bopping his tummy just a tiny bit, which he probably took as a symbol of my need to disbowel him like the Zulus do in movies, there being all that African stuff in my blood. Especially when I said Hah! and yanked out the big scissors with the red handles and held them up to show him. His eyes got a little wide. But I was already sitting on the floor going to work on my pants.

What are you doing? he said.

Cutting off my trousers.

The abuse of clothing is, of course, symbolic of the will to abuse the corporeal self.

The abuse of these pants legs is so they don't flop on my feet when I go flying past those boys' face in there on my way to a double spin reverse finger roll.

He made a yucky face. Deceit! he said. Bald deceit.

I was through with one leg and started on the other. I heard a whistle again down the hall, and the balls all stopped bouncing. Man, I had to get there!

Basketball, of all games, is the one most dedicated to physical lying, he said.

I never knew anybody who could play while lying, I said, finishing off the leg and pulling the raggedy end pieces off over my sneaks. Most people play it on their physical feet.

He said nothing. I chucked the ends in the trash can, handed him the scissors, which he winced and took with a frown, looking at them like they were a Zulu spear covered in water buffalo blood.

Thanks, Mr. E. Check you later. Keep a cool torso.

What a weary web we weave when we practice to deceive, he said, as I ran out to the hall to get in some deceive-practice. You'll see, boy—the body will be avenged for its servitude to untruth! He might have said more but I didn't hear it, for I had made it to the gym and busted in through those double doors.

I had not been thinking too much about manners and entering nicely, being half worried about what Momma would say when I came home with ruined britches and the other half worried about getting into the gym before the coach made teams up for practice games or whatever he was doing while the balls were quiet. So I just crashed in through the doors, thinking only too late that this was maybe a little reckless. And it was, too.

For there, standing at attention in a row facing me, were a dozen white boys in red and white uniforms and there, turned around to see who was busting down his doors, was this fat white man with a butch haircut wearing white shorts and a red nylon jacket with the collar turned up and a whistle in his mouth. I stopped dead. Everybody was staring hard at me. There was no sound except the doors behind me bonging as they flapped back and forth, slower and slower, until they stopped.

At first the boys' expressions had been all fearful, like the coach had been yelling at them, but they soon got relieved and then very fast got all smug and entertained. In fact a couple of them actually smiled, big private grins, like Here comes a good time.

The coach never smiled. From the start he looked peeved. He looked peeved that someone interrupted him, peeved that it was not Red Auerbach come to observe his coaching method, peeved that instead it was a black kid in ravelly corduroys and a white T-shirt. I began to think he would stare me into the floor unless I said something.

This basketball tryouts? I said. One of the boys let fall the basketball he was holding and grinned. The ball bounced itself down slowly and rolled over towards me.

No, the coach said. This is a meeting of . . . of . . . He was trying to think of something sarcastic. One of the boys helped him out.

Of the Ku Klux Klan, the boy said.

Of the Future Nurses of America, said the coach, ignoring the kid. What does it look like to you? He talked without taking the whistle out of his teeth.

Looks like I'm a little bit late to get a uniform, I said. Sorry, Coach. I was staying after with my French teacher.

Parlez-vous français? said one of the boys and for some reason all of them thought this was marvelous funny and cracked it up. His accent was awful.

You don't walk in here and just GET a uniform, said the coach. He jerked his head towards the kids with the red and white satin on. You earn the right to let your skin touch one of these.

Practice only been going for five minutes, I said. They must earn pretty fast.

He smiled. We scout the P.E. classes and know ahead of time where our talents lie. As a matter of fact, these are not what you would call open tryouts—the most promising prospects are specially invited to participate.

My P.E. class has been playing dodge ball for the two weeks since school started, I said. How is anybody supposed to see what I can do with a basketball?

He shrugged and smiled. One of the kids said, Maybe you'll be invited when the dodge ball team holds tryouts, and they all laughed.

So are you saying I can't try out for the team? I said. I bent down and picked up the ball at my feet, very casual.

I'm afraid it looks that way, the coach said, still talking around his whistle, which tooted a little with the ks at the end of looks.

Well how does this look? I said, twirling the ball in my hands and going straight up, straight as high and trim as could be, waiting until I got to the top to check out the hoop which must have been twenty-five feet away, then cradling the ball and at the last minute pulling my left hand away like Oscar Robertson and snapping that lubricated right wrist and knowing, feeling it right straight through from the tips of the fingers that had let fly the ball and touched it all the way to the last, straight down the front edge of my body to my toes just before they hit the ground again, that the shot was true, feeling the swish and tickle of the net cords rushing quick down my nerves, and landing square and jaunty in time to watch, along with everybody else, as the ball popped through the net without a single bit of deceit, so clean it kicked the bottom of the cords back up and looped them over the rim, which is called a bottoms up and means you shot it perfect and some people even count them three points in street games.

I glanced back at the coach, to find I had
been wrong. Not everybody had looked at
the ball. For some reason he had kept
staring right at me. His expression had
not changed. This flustered me a little.
Man, I had just hit a shot turned those
white boys to jelly inside, you could see it
the way they all kind of slunk at the spine
when they looked back, but this burrhead
fatso had not even bothered to check out
my act.

Nice shot, mumbled one of the white
kids, but the coach tooted on his whistle
and cut him off.

I don't think it was a nice shot, the coach
said. Not a nice shot at all.

But jeez, said another kid, Coach, cripes
it must be twenty feet. . . .

Typical jig trick shot, said the coach,
smiling a very tiny smile behind his
whistle. Fancy, one-handed, big jump.
Harlem Globetrotter stuff. You like the
Globetrotters, boy?

I like basketball, I said.

Trick stuff. Bet you can dribble behind
your back, too. Pass between your legs,
jigaboo around in the air and shoot with
your flat little nose. I bet you play a lot by
yourself. He jerked his chin at me. What
about it, Meadowlark? You play a lot by
yourself?

I play, I said, in a class by myself.

Nobody said anything. The coach chuckled softly. The boys had kind of been with me until I said that, but now I could see them straighten up again. I realized I was being a cocky nigger, true to form as Poke Peters seemed to me.

By yourself, the coach finally said, chuckling and shaking his head. Well I reckon you better get on back to your special class, then, boy, and wait until we refine our crude old five-man sport down to where we have just one-man teams. Then he turned away, picking up a ball nearby and bouncing it once, getting ready to address his troops again.

I'll play any two of you one on two, I said. If I win I get a uniform and a tryout, If I lose I go make the Harlem Globetrotters.

The coach paused, but did not turn around. He started to ignore me and go on with his lecture but about four of the white boys said Hey Coach, let me Coach, I'll take him that is me and Tom will take him Coach, and so on. They were brave as could be at the chance of a little two on one.

The coach thought for a minute. Then he turned back around and looked at me.

Pete and Vic, he said, still looking at me. Two of the boys looked startled. They had not been the volunteers. Probably too good to worry about having to impress the coach.

Yeah Coach? they said.

Pete, you take him man to man, Vic, you zone him under.

But Coach, said one of them, tall and with pimples but he had the look in his eye of a shooter, you can tell them right away.

Come on, Ace, said the other, who was Vic, and him I liked right away because he was a ballhawk like me and wanted to play just to be playing. His eyes were big and smart and he was stocky and moved like a little lion. Stop stalling and let's play him, he said, smacking Pete on the fanny. I'll even take him man to man.

Coach snapped a bounce pass at me but made it bounce right at my feet which hits you in the shins and makes you look foolish if you don't step aside, which I did and gathered it in backhand.

Game to five buckets, he said.

Nigger ball? said Vic, by which he meant make-it-take-it. Then he looked at me, blushing. Sorry, he said, I mean . . .

Nigger ball, said the Coach. Win by two.

I whipped a two-handed pass at Pete the tall one and hit him in the chest and he caught it in a hug. Shoot for outs, I said. He dribbled once and sort of looked puzzled, then shrugged and dribbled a couple more times and I saw his mind come right into focus very quick then, and he flowed a couple of steps which technically you are not supposed to when someone gives you a shot for outs but what the heck. He looked at the hoop and I knew I was right about him being the shooter for I saw the look in his eye and sure enough he pumped one up and it banked through.

Yeah, he said, smiling, let's go.

Vic took the ball out behind the line and gave me a check while the other guys sat down on the sideline. I checked it back to Vic and he started to dash off to the right. I flicked the ball with my left hand and pulled back to let him pass right by where it hung in the air, his hand still making the dribble motion, then I snatched it, threw him a head as he turned, went by him the opposite way from his motion and pulled up in Pete's face while he was still trying to figure out how you played a one-man zone. I slanted it off the glass and it zipped through. I came down and slipped around him and caught the ball as it came through the cords and was about to say One–zip when I heard the big whistle.

I looked around. The coach smiled at me. Then very slowly he raised his right hand and placed it behind his neck.

Charge, he said. We'll go the other way.

You're crazy, I said. I didn't touch him. He never even knew I was in the area. I pointed at Pete, who still looked a little puzzled.

Offense initiated contact, he said. White ball.

Asshole, I muttered, which I never curse but was mad.

That's a T, he said, tooting the whistle. Two shots. Pete?

Pete finally woke up, knowing he was to shoot. He hit both free throws.

One bucket to nothing, said the coach. White ball.

This time Vic tried to go right but I blocked him off, forcing him to use his left which most kids cannot yet do, spending most of their time only shooting. Sure enough he sort of stumbled and made a clumsy crossover and I grabbed the ball again. I was inside him so I just spun right up and popped a twelve-footer, but the whistle was blowing already as I was in the air.

That's a reach, said the Coach.

Aw, come on, no it wasn't, said Vic. It was clean, Coach. Vic was actually excited by the steal. He was a lover of the game for sure. Nice grab, he said.

Thanks, I said. But the coach had got the ball and bounced it back at Vic.

A reach, he said. Second personal. White ball.

Well, this time Vic finally got the idea he did not have to drive by me but just get the ball over to Pete for an open shot, and he did and Pete hit it from right underneath and I was down two. He did the same next time, faking the pass first and drawing me off, a nice move, then lofting it over me for a lay-up for the shooter. Three–zip. He tried the same thing next time but this time I pretended to go for the fake and backpedaled and picked Pete up before he could shoot. He went straight up without a fake and I jumped a half second later so I would be at peak just after he let it go and I was and slapped the ball away.

The whistle blew.

Hack, said the coach, shoot two.

Some of the guys on the sideline had clapped when I smacked the shot away, and now they made some Aw, come on! noises. They were okay, I suppose. Too bad they would have to play all year under the burr-head.

Pete hit both of his shots of course. Guys like him turn into beautiful robots when you give them the chance to shoot. I wonder what they do with the rest of their life. They sure don't play defense.

The coach got the ball as it dropped through from the last shot and bounced it back to Vic at the top of the key.

Coach . . . said Vic.

Play it, said the coach.

Vic looked at me and winked. Then he pretended to dribble but bounced it right into my hands. I turned and drove left behind Pete's back, he was just waiting for his next shot anyway, and flipped it in off the boards with my left hand.

The whistle blew. Pushing off, said the coach, pushing off Pete's back, we'll take it the other way.

I won't take it no way, said Vic disgusted, kicking the ball away when the coach threw it to him. The only thing he pushed off was the floor.

Get back out there Victor, said the coach, as Vic walked away to the sideline. You want to start this year?

Here's a kid could win us the city, said Vic, and nobody but you cares he's a nigger. Sorry, he said, waving at me.

Sit down, Victor, said the coach, and you won't be standing up in uniform for some time.

Maybe win us the states, he said, to the boys on the ground. They were all staring at the floor. The states, guys! The state championship! Pushing off, my ass, he said, and walked out of the gym.

We will continue as a one on one, said the coach. White ball after the foul. Shoot it, Pete, said the coach, shoving the ball at Pete over by the foul line.

Those were the magic words. I was eight feet away and didn't even try to stop it, but of course it went down anyway. That kid could shoot, I'll hand it to him. I took the ball as it came through the net, snapped a bounce pass at the coach's feet, and turned to go.

Five—nothing, white takes it, he said, as the ball banged off his shins. Take a hike, boy.

Good luck with the Globetrotters, one kid hollered as I pushed on the double doors. Nobody laughed though.

He'll probably make them, said another.

I hope so, said one more.

By then I was through, back in the hall, and the doors were bonging away. The last sound I heard from that gym was the big old scream of the whistle.

14.

Classes went along okay those first few weeks, no fuss, no fights, no friends. I was being careful, checking things out, not jumping into anything or anybody too fast. I was not lonesome or anything, having my brothers and Momma at home, though I began not to see any of my old dudes and girls now going to Parker across town, them still all together and me apart at the Nut. There had been a couple of people I met towards the end of sixth grade I thought we might get to be buds when we hit seventh, but of course we were not going to now. To make friends, you got to be around.

Most friend things happen between times. You got to be free to tag along walking home with somebody when they have been at band practice and you at hoops or in the library, and you see each other and maybe don't know much yet but like the looks and next thing you know you are walking through strange neighborhoods but it is exciting, finding someone and seeing his way home, all at once. Maybe you go in and have a couple of cookies or something, but usually not, not at first. You wave and split and think about the guy that night and see him the next day and know he was looking to see you too. Maybe that day he walks home with you, or at least partway.

You have got to be flexible too. You must say okay when someone wants to chuck the football even though you do not prefer that particular ball, or even to look at somebody's dumb bugs collection or something, which usually means it will be a limited friendship but you check those out too. If a dude says Hey, let's swap lunch, you must take what he has and swallow it smiling, even when it is something nasty like livermush sandwich and graham crackers while you are giving up a drumstick and pie. The food is not what matters.

All this stuff is important, black or white, third grade or seventh. Something catches your eye or even your ear. You may like the way a certain dude looks in his shirts or the way he sounds singing Shake A Tailfeather on the playground before school in a kickball game while waiting to get his ups. Many of my interests start in class with people. I will like the way someone talks when they are called on, or how they stand when they recite or the way they react when they do not know an answer at the board or they laugh. Mostly I am not one to go for the dudes and girls who put on the comedy show all the time, trying so hard and often quite funny but someway sad. They are too ready to be liked and like you back, while I enjoy the difficulty of seeing if I like somebody and do they like me, not setting out to attract but being careful and watching things reach between the usual gestures. One strange thing that always gets me is, if somebody writes a dynamite book report and reads it out loud. Nothing like a great book report to show somebody's class.

At Chestnut, I was just settling into my checkout. I was drawn to a few people very slightly but it is usually very slight at first, which is fine. There were all kinds of new-attraction things in French class, because the way people handled the accent operated much like the book reports always had in English, or like seeing someone shoot a pretty jump hook. We had this main pronunciation test every week. I remember the toughest one was for the hardest letter to say right in French, which is the letter r. Teacher picked one word chock-full of r and everybody had to stand up and say it out loud. The word you got was BARBARA. Man, you could look very guggly up there rolling those r sounds the wrong way in your throat, or you could look grand. One girl and one boy nailed those suckers right on the line, and I right away got interested in knowing them, all in due time. I would have, too, but the due time never came, because something very horrible took me out of friendship commission during my third week at Chestnut.

What happened was, my momma and Henri went down one day to the medical building downtown, a very old place, to see Doctor Sykes for Henri's physical which you have to get just before the first game of the football season or you cannot play, and Henri was a halfback. He got off school, Momma got off work and took him down, they had lunch at the H & W, which Henri said later was shrimp and quite good, a lot of fun, big day, all very nice.

But then when they got to the medical building Momma asked if they would play the usual game, which was this. The medical building is only four stories tall, but it has this rickety old wooden and wrought iron elevator that is slow as molasses. And starting when Maurice was a kid, my momma would always challenge us to a race up to the fourth floor where Doctor Sykes was, the kid taking the elevator by himself and Momma running up the stairs. I guess this always took our mind off getting a shot or whatever it was. It was always very much fun, and you would have Momma standing down there on the first floor landing while you got inside that old dark wood box with strange old carvings along the top and in the corners, and you would close that clackety old iron door across the front and outside Momma would pretend to be sneaking up the first few stairs for a head start and you would giggle and yell at her to stop, not fair, no Momma not yet, and she would jump back and then sneak again and you would near about collapse with giggles, which sounded very loud and peculiar inside that box by yourself. Then you would put your hand on the handle, this old leather grip I never liked to touch personally, and you would say Ready and Momma would crouch down like she was going to blast off up those stairs, and you say Set and she gets this scowl on her face and maybe puts one foot on the first step and you scream No! Then you push down on the handle, and laugh and say Go too late and Momma looks very cross and betrayed, and then the power engages and shakes the whole old box and gives you a scare but then you are going up. It is half scary, half wonderful. You pass the first landing and Momma is even and maybe

says Ha! at you. At the second landing she
is a little behind and pretending to pant a
little bit but says she will catch her wind
and beat you clean. At the third landing
you see her head coming up only as you
pass above and at the fourth you beat her.
She comes straggling up the stairs moaning and rolling her big pretty eyes and
acting like she has climbed a mountain in
high heels. You laugh so hard you don't
even know it when next thing Doc Sykes
has your britches down and jabs you with a
typhoid booster.

So on this day Momma asked if they
would play, which they had not done for
ages probably, Henri being fairly old by
now, though I still play it once in a while for
old time sake I guess as I am getting quite
old too. Well, said Henri, what about if we
switch? Momma asked what he meant and
he said he would take the stair and she
should have a chance to ride the vator.
They laughed about this switcheroo, Henri
saying he wanted to see if she really could
have beat us all those times and pretended
not to and so on. Henri remembers every
word they said, because of what happened
then.

So Momma went into the vator, laughing
and acting scared, and Henri pretended to
cheat up the steps and Momma started to
laugh like we all did and said Ready? and

Set? and then slapped that handle down with a giggle and never said Go and Henri took off up the steps. He passed her at one, was ahead of her at two and she was laughing out that it was no fair because the machine had got too old and was not as fast as it used to be, and at three he was far ahead and only just saw the top coming up. But when he got to four he saw nothing but then heard the most horrible noise and in front of him through the iron gate saw the cables shudder and then one of them went tawang and snapped and he heard Momma scream and the whole building boomed and shivered. The vator fell all four floors plus the basement and crashed bad on top of some big poles they put down at the bottom of the shaft called bumpers but the rubber that was supposed to help break the fall on them had rotted pretty much away and would not have done squat anyway.

You don't need to hear all about the rest of how they pulled Momma out and so on. Henri said it all but I could barely listen, especially after he told how Momma looked, which was she was all broken and twisted and bleeding out of both her ears. Henri can talk like that, because he is older and wants to be a veterinarian and so has to stand the sight of blood, but not me, not my momma.

I got home that day as usual, feeling good with an A on a French test, and found

Maurice and Henri moping around the house very gloomy. They told me, and I didn't cry but wanted to see Momma. They said she was in the hospital with her head shaved on account of the iron doors had crashed all over her and fractured her skull bad as could be and still stay alive. We went and saw her. She looked pretty awful and if you don't mind I'll skip it. The doctor said she would be okay though. They took care of everything and her brain was fine but she had to stay in the hospital for several weeks. He showed us the x-rays which none of us could tell beans about but he showed where the breaks were and left her brain alone. If you had asked me I would have said anything wrong up there would mean a mess forever, but thank goodness I am wrong on that one.

Anyway, naturally Momma being bad in the hospital changed our life at home right away. The three of us sat down and figured out what we would have to do to keep things rolling in the house. This was hard because we did not know every little thing that Momma had been doing when she was not at work, and we did not know where things were kept and what kind of cleaning stuff you used where and such. We found all that junk out later, but at first it was diff icult to plan everything. Still, we did it. We wrote down everything we could think of in the way of chores and duties, and we divided them up.

We saw very clearly right off that none of us would have time anymore for the things we used to do on our own, Mo with what you call troubled kids at an orphanage downtown, Henri with football, me with hoops and making new friends. We wanted to keep the home going fine, not just so we would live okay but mostly so that by the time Momma did come home we were easy and sharp at everything and so she could stay in bed and we take care of her without her feeling the need to get out of bed to help and hurt herself. We could not show any struggle if she was around at all.

So, what I got was, dinner and making lunches for everybody to take in the morning. There were other things too, like trash and raking leaves but I already did those. Cooking was new, though. I won't tell all the complicated way the divvy worked, but cooking was most convenient for me, and as nobody else knew any more than me about it, I took it. I even thought it might be fun.

It was not fun. It was a very touchy business. Things burn when you think you have hardly put any heat to them at all, and other things lie cold and wet in the pan all the while you think they are cooking away with plenty of gas. There is an awful mess to be made for the slightest sandwich.

Although we all had to eat what I cooked and suffer alike, Henri was hurt the most because he was to clean up after, and I had much trouble staying neat about the kitchen.

The first two nights we had fried eggs and toast and the third night we had Velveeta cheese melted over plain spaghetti, and then I was out of ideas for the next night so we had eggs again, only this time scrambled, a little too long. I began to wonder how I was going to make it through the weeks, much less my brothers who were both big, and needed more nourishment.

But then on the fourth day after Momma's accident I was called out of French class and sent to the office of the counselor. The counselor is this tall bony lady with large teeth very straight, and large eyes too, which are green, a color I never see in colored folk. Her hair must have been long but she wanted it to look like less, for she wadded the whole length of it up in back of her head and hung it there in a hair net that was like the bag you keep your crabs in when you fish for them off a pier in the sound. On the whole, though, she was nice enough looking.

She acted very tender toward me, like I was a bird with a broken tail or some such, so of course I knew she knew about Momma. For some reason this made me cranky and shy at the same time. I guess it was nice of her, though, and I guess I knew that somewhere deep, and made myself polite. She mumbled along for a while and then she asked did I want to talk about my mother and home situation? No, I said, thank you but I'd just as soon not. Fine, she said, very quick and agreeable, just fine. Thanks, I told her.

Then she started telling, sort of in a dreamy voice, about this family in a far off land. It was a story. It was about how this family of beavers, for that is what they were, lost their mommy beaver when a tree fell on her and found that they had to take care of their beaver dam and their river pool all by their courageous little self, gnawing down trees and finding water vegetables and making their nice vegetable beaver pies and oh so many things. And it was very, very hard and they had to grow up in so many ways so very, very fast.

Never trust anyone who says very, very, because you are only supposed to say it once and twice means they are trying to put something over on you or else are stupid. This counselor was not stupid but she must have thought I was. When she stopped to take a breath, before going into how the littlest beaver got so frustrated trying to make his beaver pies the right way, I cut her off sharp and said, We do just fine for ourselves.

What? she said, coming down hard out of beaverland.

We are doing just fine all by ourselves at home. We don't need anyone to notice us, thank you.

She pressed her lips together and nodded hard. Then she switched to shaking her head and said, But like the little beavers, don't you think you could use someone to—

No, I said.

You see, the beavers let Mr. and Mrs. Muskrat come and take care of—

No, I said. Nobody comes to help. No.

She clammed up at that, and sat staring at me. A couple of times she started to say something but I frowned because I could see she was still on the beaver kiddie kick. She sat back and stared again. Then, finally, in a sudden blurt, talking not in her dreamy voice but straight up, she said, Okay, buster, how's about you learn to cook here at school?

Now you're talking, I said.

She broke into all kinds of a smile at that and went on talking fast to say what she had in mind. What it was is sticking me in a Home Economics class. These are usually all girls, learning how to bake cakes for the handsome men they will marry if they are lucky. You can hear them giggling when they yank their goodies out of the oven because the Home Economics cooking room is down the hall from where French meets and I hear them playing with pots and stuff though never smelled food yet. But I figured I could pick up some tips. I figured dudes must be able to learn as well as girls how to knock some food together, though nobody usually thought to teach us. I mean, our hands don't grow a certain peculiar way makes them unable to grasp a spatula or an oven knob. Anyway, anything would help, and the sooner the better. It was going to be spaghoots and melted cheese again tonight.

The counselor told me I could drop into the Home Ec class, which is what she called it, quite easily. It was a mere formality of dropping the class that met during Home Ec period.

Okay, I said. Then I froze. I remembered: I always heard the kitchen noise jive during French class, therefore that meant I was going to have to drop French!

Wait! I said, but she was already filling out a form and talking.

Home Ec meets at two different times, third period and fifth. Let's see, if we drop you out of French . . .

No! I said.

She looked up, startled. What's wrong?

I don't want to drop French.

You . . . What do you mean, you don't want to drop French? She looked truly amazed.

I want to keep it. It is my favorite subject.

She wrinkled up her forehead and looked a little annoyed. But it's so hard! All those verbs. I NEVER liked French.

But I do, I said. I like it fine, I even like the verbs.

She looked at the schedule. But . . . if you don't drop French fifth period, that means you'll have to drop Communications! She said it as if this was the craziest thing she ever heard.

Shucks, I said, but I guess I have to sacrifice. That will do it. Communications has to go. I was trying hard not to holler Hooboy and toss in a couple of significant hand gestures to express my delight.

Her forehead got even more wrinkled. But . . . surely you don't want to drop Com. Surely!

Then her eyes got a little woozy and her cheeks got a little pink and she looked up at the corner of the ceiling and started slowly waving one of her hands, back and forth, very soft like conducting a real religious choir or something. In her old dreamy voice, but different too, she said, Don't you find Chuck Egglestobbs to be the most completely elegant sensibility you have ever met?

She had it bad. I let her wave and swoon for a couple of minutes, and then, not wanting to make her mad enough to force me out of French, I said, Well, he can sure use the body!

She turned red and stopped waving her hand and glared at me, still looking kind of eager all the same. Young man, she said, what do you mean to say?

You know, he communicates with his knees and feet and such.

Ah, she said, yes, of course. Yes, you are right. Hmm. He—and here she got moony again—he certainly conveys himself with the utmost physicality.

We sat for a minute in silence, her dreaming of Egglestobbs and his talking knees, me thinking hard of how to get her away from thinking good things about old Com and yet keeping her in a soft mood enough to let me have my way and drop it. I tried, but the only way out was the melodrama. So I squinched up in my chair to look thin and sorrowful, and talked a little higher than usual and with more breath in it.

Body language is no good, I sighed, if your body is wasting away. I . . . I want so very, very much to feed my brothers.

She woke up and turned those big eyes on me and watched me pout and got so saddened up that I felt terrible and ashamed of myself. But it worked. She

said, Oh, yes, young man. That is very
dearly put. Oh my.

Then, pausing a couple of times to look
up at me with six kinds of pity, she signed
my slip.

I was out of Com. I was dans le français.
And I was going to be a Home Economist.

15.

I was out in the hall already walking back
to French when the counselor called me. I
turned around and she said, I forgot to tell
you. You will be glad to know that you are
not the only boy in the Home Ec class.

For some reason, I was not especially
glad to hear this. In fact I got a little
annoyed. I think I was getting kind of at-
tached to being an only. The only smarty in
advanced math, the only black kid in
Chestnut, the only boy in Home Ec. So I
just shrugged and looked at her like what
else did she have to say?

There's . . . there is another boy, that is,
she said, wrinkled up again.

I guess you said so, I said. She stood looking at me, obviously thinking about the
other kid.

His name is Braxton Rivers the Third,
she said. That is the poor thing's name.

I said, Yeah, you got to feel sorry for

someone stuck with Braxton the Third. Sounds like one of my people.

She blushed. I was not referring to his rather dignified name when I expressed sympathy, she said. Then she shook her head and started to step back into her office.

Why? I said. Why is he a poor thing? Has his momma been dropped down an elevator and crushed by wrought iron, down four floors bleeding out both ears? Has she? Does she have her head all broken up? She going to be in the hospital for weeks with a shaved head and who knows if there might be damage to the brain? I was cheating a little there, having been assured by the doctor, but for some reason I was feeling mad and sorry for myself and even maybe jealous. The counselor looked at me straight and frowned and I knew I was starting to deserve it if she treated me a little like a child, but she didn't.

No, she said. No, it isn't like that. Not exactly anyway.

Lucky him, I said, very cocky.

She stared at me for a long moment. We'll see, she said. Then she closed the door.

16.

The first day in Home Economics was trying on aprons. No kidding.

I walked in ten minutes late on account of being lectured to (in words this time) by old Chuck Egglestobbs when he signed my slip to drop his class. He told me I had a long way to go to get my body's truth under control, especially if I kept perverting its natural instincts by forcing it into fakery in the name of athletics. I almost invited him to come check out my fakery in a little one on one, but I knew he would give me no credit for all the grace in the world if it did not fit in with his theories. Anyway, I was a couple of minutes late.

First thing I saw was the teacher, standing up on a kitchen table holding up a loud red apron with white spots and ruffles. She waved it at this whole room full of girls and then tilted her hips and pressed the apron up against herself all slinky, saying A garment, girls, it's a garment not a towel. She stopped dead when she saw me walk in, and she stared at me, still pressing the garment to her hips and holding her mouth open. She had a bunch of makeup on, and her lips were a reddish orange that made you sick when you saw it so close to the pinky-red apron. The girls stared at me too. There must have been twenty of them and they all had garments of their own, holding them up to their hips.

Hi, I said. Is this the place where a fellow can learn how to wear his apron?

That broke them up, all except the teacher, who just looked puzzled and said, You must be the boy.

I must be, I said. (I did not mean to be too snappy, but I get sort of jaunty sometimes when I am a little nervous, and those girls all looked old and large and they stared at you like you were a fly in their new-made vanilla pudding.)

We . . . we have another boy, she said, kind of like she could only take one at a time.

I heard, I said.

He is absent today, she said. He has the flu.

No, a virus, said one of the girls.

What? said the teacher.

A virus, please, Miss Pimton. In home room they said he was sick on account of a virus.

Influenza is a virus, said Miss Pimton, a little testy. However, that need not concern us too much, does it? Now, young man. What did you say your name was?

Jerome Foxworthy.

A few girls laughed.

All right Jerome. She looked confused. Ahm . . . Matty Sue, where does . . . ahm . . . our other boy sit?

A girl in a yellow dress holding a blue plaid apron pointed at the back table where there was nobody sitting today.

That's where, said Matty Sue, wrinkling herself up and making faces and all the girls laughed. I got the idea this other dude had been having a hard time getting himself liked in Home Ec. Probably he didn't look good in an apron.

Thank you. Then I think Jerome . . . or shall I call you Jerry?

No.

Oh. All right, Jerome. Then I think you had best sit back where . . . ahm . . .

Braxton, said one of the girls.

Thank you. Where Braxton will sit upon his return. We work in partners here. I think it would be best if you and he were partners. Unless Matty Sue objects, as she is Baxter's partner at temporary present.

Braxton, I corrected, but nobody noticed.

No ma'am, said Matty Sue, I don't object one iota.

I bet you don't, said one of the girls and Matty Sue made like wiping sweat off her head and went Whew! and everybody laughed, except me. I was feeling pretty sorry for this other kid, and glad at least we could team up as long as these girls were on the attack.

I walked back to that table and put down my books. Everybody watched me. Most of the girls and the teacher still held their aprons up to themselves. I stood there and finally they saw I wasn't going to do anything more than just stand there being black and a boy and so they started looking back at the teacher.

She sort of shook herself awake, and looked at her watch and said, Okay girls, I guess it's time to clean up for the day. This meant that it was time for the girls to stuff their aprons in their table drawers and then talk nonstop for fifteen minutes until the bell, having to unwind after a hard lesson, and there being nothing within sight to clean up.

I wondered when the cooking was going to start. I couldn't satisfy Maurice and Henri by strutting around looking sharp in an apron.

17.

Over that weekend at home we ate mostly corn bread made from the box recipe and a canned ham our next door neighbor Mrs. Paul gave us, but I told the brothers about Home Ec and talked it up big, promising that the cook was going to fly come Monday night. I did not tell them about the apron jive. I wanted them to believe in Home Economics. Maybe then the stuff I made would not taste as bush, being officially taught stuff.

When I got to class on Monday, I did not look straight back at the table where I was to sit, but when I slung the eyes up for a charming smile at Miss Pimton who did not know where to look but not in my eyes, I could see out the corners that there was someone sitting there. I still did not look, turning toward the back and nodding at a couple of those dippy girls who giggled and fussed getting their polka dots on straight.

But I started to feel a twiggle in my stomach.

I was feeling a little cocky, still. It was the same sort of feeling of having my onlyness broken that I had felt talking in the hall to the counselor. I did not like it, I knew it was foolish, but I could not help it and I knew I was not going to give that dude an easy time. Jerome can be cool and snappy when he is bad, and I felt like I was going to be bad. All the same, I was really pretty excited—here was a boy I would almost have to get to know, all alone like we were in that institute of wives for the future. I knew something was waiting for me back there in that kid, as I walked closer, swinging a cool checkout glance his way. But my cool fell right off my face, and I gaped. Sitting there, looking very different out of uniform but still the same kid without doubt, was the shortstop. What was it his momma called him? Bix. Bix Bix Bix. Bix for Braxton. Bix my baseball main man, my mystery opponent in phantom one on one, my new partner in cookery.

I expected him to recognize me and he did not, shooting me only a very timid don't-hurt-me look with a half smile like inviting me to be friendly, and then looking down again. Then I realized he could not have recognized me—he had never seen me before. This made me snooty again, like he someway SHOULD have got to know me while I was in the crowd watching him or something. Man, I was not thinking too clearly in the feelings that day.

I stared at him and he just looked down, feeling the stare and not wanting to meet it. I checked him out pretty thorough, and saw that he really was pretty different now, different from what I would have thought that Bix who gave me shivers pivoting on the double play and whipping that arm would be. First of all, I saw that kid as being sure of himself enough to look anybody in the eye and take the check-out proudly. Not this look-down dude here. Second, and maybe here I thought Egglestobbs' way for a moment, I thought he would be holding himself tight and high and clever on his feet, moving sure and fast and giving off that glow with all of his grace. But no, he slunk all down like the white basketball boys after I hit that boss shot, only he had no reason to. I had taken no shots yet.

He was a good looking kid, despite being a white boy with the usual problem of they have no good tone in the skin. He had thick light hair kind of long for most whites, but instead of hanging down it sort of bushed out, wavy enough not to be bristly. From that one glance I saw his eyes were very fine, round and big, the same light brown color as his hair which was a little odd but in a good way. I liked his eyebrows, very thick. I liked his cheek bones too, they stuck out like mine only higher and right now they were pale which most white people have red on them. The weirdest thing about the face was this pink flush in the forehead, not a scar or anything, just like what most whites get when they blush only in a different place and irregular. Later I found out he got it his first time up in a Little League game, age eight, when a twelve-year-old kid pitching beaned him smack in the thinker. But it only ever turned pink when he was ashamed or shy and never showed on the surface or at other times.

His clothes were naturally different from his spiffy uniform, but even so I expected they would be just as sharp. At first I thought he was just a mess in bad threads, but then I noticed that the clothes actually were good things. Nice cord pants and a yellow button-down like I like, and a tweed jacket, which would have looked fancy worn the right way with a little confidence. Nice duds. But right now they were only being used to carry around a very grand set of wrinkles, baby. This boy had not seen an iron in moons. What was wrong with his momma, she let him get out the house like this?

Then I felt a little tingle. His momma—what was he doing in Home Ec? I looked fast at his shoes. Leather loafers, all polished very nice. Wrinkly good clothes, polished good shoes. These added up, along with the counselor's talk the other day, and told me: something was wrong with this boy's mother too.

Here is how it figured. First, good threads. That went along with his momma, snazzy and decked out in full class to watch a ball game and yet not look silly either. Nice shoes, too. Now, what do you learn from polished shoes plus wrinkled clothes? Just this: a kid always polishes his own shoes, but his momma always irons his clothes. So if his shoes are done, it means he is still trying to look okay, well trained or whatever; but if his clothes are messy it means no momma at the ironing board, and nobody either to check his state of appearance before he gets it out the door for school in the a.m. Hey—maybe this kid has no daddy too, I thought.

On the whole it was no wonder the girls treated him creepy. He was like a pup begging you not to kick him and girls like that cannot resist getting a foot on such helplessness.

I sat down, and said, So, man, you going to be my partner?

I guess we are, he said. I mean, I guess I am.

You here to learn to sling the pots?

He looked at me puzzled.

You know, I said, sling the pots, fling the pans—cook, man.

Oh, he said, sure. He grinned, then looked down. Sling the pots, fling the pans, he said. Or if not, open cans.

Hey, I said, that's not bad. Open those cans. Only we probably don't learn how to get into a can until next semester, after apron tying and rubber glove putting on and choosing the right smell of dish soap and a sponge to go with your nail polish.

He shrugged. He had livened up for a second, but now he was back to being pure fish. I looked up toward the front, sighing. He just hunkered down. Between Miss Pimton and this dude, I might have a very trying time in old Home Ec.

Miss Pimton acted like she heard my thought, and set right out to obey. For she got out some tubs of water and a laundry basket full of torn up newspaper and smiled and said Okay girls, today, and tomorrow too, plenty of time, we are going to do patties.

Patties! squealed the girls, clapping their hands.

What do you think the newspapers are for? I asked Bix.

Newspaper patties? he said. I laughed, but he was right. For Miss Pimton made us come around her table and proceeded to show us how to make that perfect patty for the grill or broiler, only it was out of paper mache. Wet shredded newspaper, just right for the coals. Just right for tonight's supper at the Foxworthy household. Here we are, Maurice—you get last week's front page, and Henri, knowing your thing for football I have pattied up the sports section. Looked like fried eggs once more for the boys.

And I did not know, but when the next week we finally started on our first edible project, as Miss Pimton called it, I was in for the worst sight yet of White Man's Nonsense. I was never so amazed as when she told us what we were going to cook up. I mean, the usual jive like Communications of making something that seems important out of nothing is bad enough. But making something out of nothing and then EATING it . . .

18.

1/2 cup milk
1/2 cup water (warm)
2 teaspoons cinnamon
1 cup sugar
2 1/2 cups crushed Ritz crackers
1 pie crust

There you go. That's the ticket. Mix it all together, stick it in the oven, and you get yourself one official yummy Home Economic style Mock-Apple Pie. Dig it.

Mocking apples, man. Where did somebody get the idea that this was a good way to spend the day? Miss P thought it was pure genius. So did the girls. Imagine! Making something that looked and tasted a little bit like apple pie, only it was all completely fake! Hooray! How smart everybody in this world is!

I was groaning after it hit me that Miss Pimton was truly serious, but I was drowned out. Oh boy I bet that dumb old

Buck Taylor will eat this up and never tell in a million years, or Sakes alive that high and mighty old Skeeter Darby won't he be fooled but good? All the girls clapped and begged could they take some to their boyfriends, PLEASE? Miss Pimton loved it. She smiled like she was the queen giving the secrets of high life to all the people on feast day. Yes, she said, every team would prepare a pie, and they would get baked and we could take them to whomever we wanted. She looked at Bix and me when she said this with her eyes full of important meaning. I realized she was thinking we would actually take this tricky glop home and feed it to our poor starving families, bless our poor undernourished little hearts.

I couldn't stand that look, so I spoke up. What do I want to go fooling my brothers with a bunch of yellow crackers in water for? I said.

She looked startled. This food—

This is not food, I said. It's a costume. The only reason anybody even thinks about apple pie when they eat this is the cinnamon, I bet, because they are used to tasting cinnamon in real apple pie, and you are counting on fooling them on this little decoration taste alone. You're probably right, most of these dopes (I almost said Most of these white dopes but I held back but I think Miss Pimton knew, for she

blushed something awful) will go no further than tasting the spice and saying Ah,
this must be apple pie, because most dopey
people judge too fast from the first thing
they see anyway. So you put some little
thing in to trick them, and it's enough. But
you can't fool the body needing vitamins
can you?

Miss Pimton blushed hard and cleared
her throat very high several times. The
girls were hanging open at the mouth and
not yet recovered enough to look hateful at
me, which they did soon enough. I was
showing my true colors at last, what they
knew I must be like all along, uppity and
loud and rude.

Miss Pimton finally said, trying to be
dignified and patient but sounding only
quivery, Mock-Apple Pie, Jerome, is actually delicious in its own way.

More delicious than apple pie? snapped a
voice beside me and I jumped and looked
around and, whew, there he was! The
shortstop was back! I mean, Bix had perked
up his spine and stuck out his chin a bit and
his cheeks were red and eyes flashing. He
looked about ready to take a nasty one-
hopper to his right backhand and whip it to
first off the back foot beating the runner by
six steps and killing the rally cold. I said,
My man! very soft, and maybe he heard me
but did not show it, looking very hard at

Miss Pimton, not letting her off, almost that look that comes before a smile on his face. He knew he had her. So did she. She was bad surprised that he had waked up from being the puppy.

Well, I—

Come on. Is it tastier, more delicious, more scrumptious than old genuine apple pie, old Non-Mock-Apple-Pie?

I checked out the girls. They were gaping again, this time at Bix.

Well, Braxton, said Miss Pimton, fidgeting with her glasses on her nose, I suppose, no, that Mock-Apple Pie has not quite the richness of apple pie, but . . . for beginners—

Why make it, then?

Well . . . some people find that—

Are Ritz crackers more nourishing than apples?

Well, I don't believe, no, I could not think they are—

Are they less expensive? Do they save on the family grocery bill in these difficult times?

She mumbled. Man, he was pressing. He walked over and snatched the cracker box and brought it back to our table.

Seventy-six cents for ten ounces, he read. I think apples go for about twenty cents a pound. So Ritz crackers are not more economical for the home, are they?

I could not believe this was the same slouchy dude. Do it, baby, I said. The girls glared.

It appears that the crackers are a bit more costly, Miss Pimton admitted, all defeated.

So, he said. Not more scrumptious, not more nourishing, not cheaper. So why in the blue do we have to make this junk?

Everybody just sat there looking their own bad looks. Bix watched Miss Pimton. The girls did too. Miss Pimton sort of cringed and frowned and glanced back at Bix from time to time. Nobody said anything. Finally, I said, I'll tell you why we have to make it.

Bix turned around, surprised but interested. Miss Pimton looked relieved and actually said Why? like she really wanted to know too. Then she blushed and tried to look like she just wanted to hear how silly my reason was. The girls were ready for more nonsense to scoff at.

It's simple, I said. We have to make this crummy pie just because we CAN make it. That's all. That's the reason a lot of fools do a lot of things. Some joker thought of doing this one day, and he did it, and then it was on the books as something that COULD be done and so people have to keep on doing it.

Then I thought to myself, That is white man's disease, thinking you must do whatever you can dream up just because you're so smart. And it is black man's disease to wish they had the same inclination.

Everybody just sat for a few minutes, Miss Pimton looking about to bawl, the girls starting to strut back and forth putting on their aprons and asking could they start please Miss P? because THEY really WANTED to make this YUMMY pie and couldn't wait to share it with their dearest loved ones, and now wouldn't she show them how to mash up these old crackers just right, please? And could they be daring and maybe use just a little extra cinnamon or sugar because that Mick Hogan just LOVED sweet things.

I looked around at Bix. He was watching the girls and Miss Pimton, frowning. He was not as hot and bright as a few minutes ago, still tough but hurt too, seeing that the girls were actually going to keep business going as usual. Already Miss Pimton was coming back to form, starting to warm up as she took a bowl from Matty Sue who was trying to look all clumsy and needing help, and commenced to show the dear girl a few key tricks probably her momma taught her about mashing crackers just right like they did in colonial times. Bix looked over at me. His eyes were all sunk, like as to say They have beaten us have they not, partner? I looked back at him hard and hot as like to say Not a bit, brother, not us, not with such a measly thing as a pie full of wet crackers. We stared into each other's eyes there for a long time, heat growing and light moving very sure between us, and it was great, grand in the chest and fluttery in the stomach as we forgot everything else and took each other to each. I don't remember feeling the smile start to come on my face or noticing it start on his, but suddenly I felt my cheeks hurt and saw his smile too, and my eyes had those good tears that stay inside, his too, I think. We knew each other could do anything together.

Hey, he said, grinning very crafty.

I get you, I said.

As long as we got to make one of these mock jessies—

We got to make the very mockingest!

The most chock-full of mock!

The mock de la mock! I said, knowing French.

Get a bowl, he said, and keep an eye on my wrist work while I mash.

Only, I said, if you pay the closest attention to my handsome cinnamon technique.

Don't use too much, he said. Johnny Mack Fathead does not love cinnamon and may be offended.

And be watchful of the sugar, I said, for Arnold T. Stomachface is known to be not partial to sweets.

We laughed, and got the junk to make our pie. The girls had already started and were all gritting their teeth at work. They did not hear a word we said.

I was very happy. I had just gotten myself a best bud. I was positive about that, I really thought so.

19.

We flew on the pie. Miss Pimton was popeyed when she cruised past our table once and gave a look, expecting to see probably a bloaty mess of dough but instead there was the cleanest, sharpest mock pie she had ever inspired in any of the long line of Home Ec students who had mashed a cracker for her. She snuck over again a minute later, wrinkling the forehead. It was plain ours was a hundred times the pie any girl had made. Bix and I were putting on a show, laying these little twists on the edge of the crust very fancy, even pricking the letters M-A on the top, like the pies in stores have so you can tell which kind it is, P for peach and C for cherry and such except for French apple which you don't need initials because it has icing and everyone can see that.

The girls had suggested a sort of friendly contest with Miss Pimton picking the best pie and that would be the one we would bake first. What an honor.

Well, it was plain as ike to Miss P that the boys were sitting pretty in the great pie mock-sweepstake. We did not give a hoot but all the same it would be good to show the girls that you could make the best cracker pie even if you hated the very idea, and surely anything you can do that with cannot mean much. Bix and I did not say anything like this to each other but I think we must have felt the same.

Miss Pimton finally decided the contest was going to be anonymous, with all of the class together picking the best pie from all of them lying on the big table away near the oven, without knowing whose was which. So whenever anyone finished their pie she carted it over away in the corner and shuffled it into the arrangement. The girls were a little disappointed, but this way at least they could each pretend not to recognize their own pie and think theirs was the one picked, and nobody would have to know.

Well, they thought they could pretend that. But when time came to gather round and select the lucky pie, they all knew each to herself she did not make that sharp pie that was picked unanimously. They shot a few suspicious mean eyes around, like they had been betrayed. They never looked at us, though. Until just before the pie was popped into the heat. A few of them suddenly realized who put that gorgeous hunk of crackers together, and gaped. We grinned back, but very cool. The ones who knew said nothing, rathering to die than let on they had been hustled by two negative dudes.

We all cleaned up while the pie was baking. Nobody said much. After a while Miss Pimton yanked the pie out, and there it was, fresh jive pie.

Now, said Miss P with a mischief look, now, shall we try a little test and see how good we are?

Oh no! said Bix's voice behind me, very soft but suddenly different and fearful. I was surprised and looked around at him. He was frowning, did not look at me straight, staring up at Miss Pimton. He flicked his eyes at me then, and the look was like saying What? What is this? I don't like this. He was slipping back fast into the slinker, right while I watched. His eyes kept getting deeper in their holes and looking more confused.

What . . . no, he said. He watched Miss Pimton hold up a finger to the girls like to say Wait just a sec, and then step out into the hall. No, Bix said, still so soft nobody but me could hear and I think I was even not supposed to. Too far, he said.

What is it, man? I said. He did not look at me or say anything, just frowned deeper when Miss Pimton came back into the room dragging along this teacher by the arm.

Class, she said, this is Mr. Spearman. He just happened to be walking by, and I invited him in for . . . a piece of pie!

The girls all squealed under their breath and tried to keep from laughing and nudged each other like Oh boy this is going to be good! The dude was doing his best to look slightly confused but obliging, smiling with his mouth closed and nodding to the class and very casual, just happened to be strolling down the hall in the middle of the period and my yes a piece of pie sounded delightful. You could see with one eye that he was acting, even if you could not figure out the whole setup, which a two-year-old could. But not those girls, man, they wanted to believe. Tee hee, they poked each other.

We just baked this pie, said Miss Pimton, and we wonder would you be so good as to taste it for us?

Certainly, said the man. Then he looked at us and raised his eyebrows and lit up his eyes and said, Yum! He actually said that word, Y-U-M. The girls loved it. I snorted.

Don't, please, said Bix. I turned around. He had slunk back to a chair near the back wall, and he was kind of drooping there, looking miserable.

Hey, Braxton, I said, what is it, man?

Shh, said the girls. Bix said nothing, staring straight ahead. I looked back up front.

Miss Pimton had cut the pie and laid out a steaming slice on a plate. Mr. Spearman took a fork from her and cut off a bite, and then jabbed it with his fork. He held it up in front of his face and closed his eyes and made a big cartoon sniff, saying MMMM! The girls made all kinds of funky puppy noises keeping from giggling until they almost died from how smart they were, tricking this dude. As for me, I was thinking I had seen many a more believable scene on Crusader Rabbit than all of this weak-headed crapola.

Well, said the mock-sucker, I guess I just have to give in and taste this pie. Can't resist anymore.

He looked like he could still resist a good while longer, for to tell the truth he was beginning to look sorry he had whacked off such a big bite, but he gulped and popped it into his mouth and chewed, wrinkling his forehead and nodding while doing so, to show how hard he was concentrating on the deliciousness of the whole experience. He made little grunty noises, URM! URM! all the while every now and then, nodding and indicating he was really knocked out by the splendor. The girls were stuffing sweater sleeves and pigtail ends into their mouth to keep from howling. Miss Pimton gave us a big wink from behind the poor guy's shoulder.

Finally he swallowed it with a quick huge gulp.

Ah, he said. Boy oh Boy.

Please, no, it's too much, too bad, hissed Bix behind me, but nobody paid mind.

Do you like our pie? said Miss Pimton.

Oh yes, certainly yes, he said, nodding like his neck had just broke and he wanted to make sure. Oh heavens what a pie it is.

Miss Pimton looked out at the girls and smiled. Then she said to the dude, Tell me, what kind of pie IS that?

The dude acted like this was the most natural question in the world for him to be asked, as if maybe the contents of the pie had just slipped our minds twenty minutes after we made it, and he was glad to fill us in. Why, he said, getting ready for his big line, it is the most tasty apple pie I ever—

He did not finish because all of the girls whooped it out on this one, letting go all of their wonderful tricksy stuffed-up pride at how foxy they all were to make such a thing and have this new power and screaming and hugging and clapping. What fun it was going to be as a genuine home economist doing such things all the livelong day for their puzzled families. They whooped up Miss Pimton too, her standing there with her hands clasped in front, her head tilted to one side, beaming in pride and modesty at them, taking their joy in and being the modest mother of all this smart accomplishment. After a minute she nodded and said, or at least her lips moved though you could hear nothing, Girls girls. Then she clapped her hands a few times, looking around, nodding and smiling at each of them, Girls girls.

But then all of a sudden she stopped dead. Her face went white and her mouth drooped and her eyes got wide and scary. Her hands stopped in the middle of a clap forgotten in front of her, held together like she had caught a bee and it was stinging her hands like fury but she was too frozen in pain to let go. All the girls suddenly shut up, seeing her. The dude could not see, and continued to nod and blush, still trying to look not in on the joke. Finally he got curious at the silence and turned to look at Miss Pimton, then got very serious and shot his eyes back where she was looking. With that, we all turned and looked, for she was staring at the back of the room.

It was Bix. He was standing on a chair in the back corner. He was slunk against the walls and he kept nudging them with his elbows, like to make sure he was still there, keeping touch, while he stared out at the room. His breath was fast and almost like crying, but no tears ran out of those eyes. They looked too hard for tears. They were mad and fast, flicking around the faces, open wide, white and red like marsh-mallows on fire. He was upset, you would almost think out of control, but there was anger in there and nobody is ever out of control as long as they are mad about some-thing, you can tell that from watching kids throw tantrums, they only go over the edge when they forget what they want. Bix looked like he wasn't forgetting. Lies, he said.

Like everybody I had taken a step back when I turned and saw him fierce back there, but now I stepped up and then took another couple closer to him.

Hey man, I said.

Braxton, said Miss Pimton, but then she just stood there and shivered.

Come on, man, I said, it's okay, knowing that whatever it was was not okay at all.

Bunch of liars, said Bix, very clear, not like a quivery mess at all but someone very sure of himself.

Young man, said Mr. Spearman, listen young man—

SHUT UP! yelled Bix. NOBODY IS TELLING THE TRUTH! The man started to say something again and Bix laughed and shouted APPLE PIE MY ASS! He grabbed one hand with the other and started scratching it with his nails, very hard. You should not lie, he said.

Baxter, now, said Mr. Spearman, looking quick at Miss Pimton to see if he had the name right, but she wasn't paying him any heed. Now listen, Baxter—

You won't get away with lies, Bix said, very clear. He was scratching his hand but not noticing and he had started to bleed from a picked place. A couple of the girls had started to make little whimpers staring at him, they were so scared and did not expect such a thing because of a little fake pie trick and had no idea what was happening to this boy. I did not either but I knew nobody else would help him out of it so I took a couple more steps and said Hey, Bix, which I called him for the first time, having not been told it by him but picked it up only from his momma at that game, not really having the right to use it but that was how I had thought of him all that time.

It turned out to be the right thing, because he looked at me when I said it and watched me come. His face was slowly untwisting but still angry but not at me. Bix, man, I said, it is all right, absolutely we are going to be okay now.

I'm not crazy, he said, like he was disgusted with me talking down to him. But they are lying lying lying.

I agree, I said. He was still scratching at that hand and shaking now and then, and while I stepped closer a drop of blood slung off and caught me smack on the lip and before I knew I reflex licked the wet on my lip. It tasted so strange I shuddered but was not like to be sick or anything.

I took the last couple of steps over, his eyes on me all the time, and then I put out my hands and took his apart. He relaxed them as soon as I touched them, and looked down like he had not realized what he was doing. His blood on the one hand was warm. It did not exactly give me the creeps or anything but all the same I did not like that it was on the outside and not back in where it belonged.

He looked at me, mad still but sinking, and said You got to tell them, man, because you know it's wrong. They can't get away with this lying shit. Tell them it's crackers and water.

They know, I said.

They can't get away with it, he said, pulling back a little at first when I tried to help him down off the chair but then giving up.

It's just a trick, I said.

It's two tricks, he said, it's a million lies and they can't make me a part of it. It's us tricking him and him tricking us back and tricks and lies, and soon it's gone and nobody knows the truth and you can go crazy in there.

Don't go crazy in there, Bix, I said.

They are . . . they . . . some people, they— But he didn't finish the sentence, frowning hard and really dropping into the slink now as he got tired fast, but stopping and looking out at all of them staring at us, the girls white and deadfaced and never thinking this could go with dotted aprons and oven heat and the nice crispy sound of crackers mashing in the home. Bix stared back for a second and held it. They dropped their eyes, and then he leaned on me and I led him to the door.

Oh man, he said, I don't know.

I didn't know too. I walked him down to the nurse's office. He was back to himself pretty much by the time we got there and went straight to a cot and fell asleep and I sat on the edge while he slept. Nobody bothered us. We smelled like cinnamon and blood. Cinnamon blood brothers.

THIRD PART

20.

Bix was not in school for the whole next week. Miss Pimton told us he had left Home Ec class and I could work alone without a partner if I wanted or she could set up a shuffle of the girls to partner me in shifts a couple of weeks a throw, the idea being obvious that no one would want to get stuck with me forever. I said I would work alone and very glad to do so. Actually, I kind of regretted it. The girls all acted more like human beings after Bix's bad day, with less playacting of joy at the well-made patty (hamburger this time) and no giggling at all, and generally more businesslike. We started right away making real food, burgers first and then the next week a chicken and biscuits with gravy from the pan the chicken cooked in.

For those few weeks I did not know what had become of Bix. I thought at first several times of going by his house if I could find out from the office where he lived. But then I was getting pretty busy with my cooking at home. I found out that learning to cook does not save you time. Cooking the right way takes much more than cooking slapdash. The difference is just that what you make is good, instead of trash. I had to go to the market after school most days, never shopping for more than one or two days, which was all I could carry and us with no car. Once I got home with the groceries, I had to start right away if I was to make a good dinner, having about two hours which it took all of, most times. I got so I could follow a recipe even for things we had not made in Home Ec, because once you use a few recipes in class you begin to see how they work and what all the abbreviations mean and you get a sense of timing. The more I practiced the better the meals, until Mo and Henri were really excited every night to see what Jerome snazzed up for dinner, such as Mexican Meat Loaf and Chicken Dumplings and one night a Vegetable Curry which comes from India and quite spicy. We all like spicy food except for Momma, so we might as well dig it while she is gone.

Then, after those few weeks, I never quite got the chance to see about Bix because the biggest surprise happened one day, which was Momma came home early from the hospital, in the ambulance, but no siren, her being just fine and only along for the ride. She was doing her recovery faster than they thought, and so they let her go. The doctor called Maurice and gave him all kinds of instructions on what she needed checked and done for her, which Maurice wrote down very serious and nervous, including even things like IF BANDAGES GET DIRTY, CHANGE THEM which any fool could know without writing it down. Momma was herself but very softly so, and plus she was wearing this turban of gauze bandaging and looked quite cute actually, though it sounds horrible to say like that. Mo lost the list right away, but we took care of her fine.

We were all very happy, of course. Momma had a million questions and could not believe how we had taken care of things and each other, and we acted so casual about it all like of course there had never been any doubt. Maurice was very serious and pulled out these secret charts he had kept on Henri and me, full of Crises Averted and Challenges Met and Orientations Adjusted and all kinds of his jive, to show that, yes, we were doing okay. Momma laughed so hard when she saw it that we all knew she was doing okay too, even Maurice finally joining in with us howling, though he expected her to take it all very solemn like the queen getting the secret documents from the spy. He left the chart for her to study at her leisure, he said. There was supposed to be a graph to go along with it, but he lost it. Henri found it later when sweeping under the bed and he threw it away.

Those days were wonderful. Momma was home. We all found out how well we could make things on our own, better even than when there was only the brothers there, because now we were using that practice to keep everything perfect and it counted for more than just us getting by. At first Momma was trying to get her hands in, to get back involved, but we did not let her and soon she watched while all the things she saw about the home were done just right.

Momma got along pretty okay with her healing up. The bandages came off in a couple of weeks and her hair started growing back in these little fuzzy tufts made her look like a six-year-old. She talked more and more like she always did, though softer, for she always had a little bit of headache and would for a while I guess. Henri and Maurice talked all the time when the three of us were cleaning up after dinner or something about how great she was and how it was fine to see she was back to herself. But I was not so sure yet.

There was only one thing I was worried about, and that was whether she had gotten a little of her smarts knocked out. I did not think so, and I did not draw my worry from anything she showed or did. I drew my worry from knowing how fragile all the ways of being intelligent are. So many things whizzing around in there, ideas and quickness and a smell for the truth, all hooking up the right way to make you do the things you do right. I couldn't help think a crash like Momma's would maybe bust a few quicknesses, cut some of the sense for truth, and you would not be able to notice what was not there any longer. Shifts and misses, you do not see them for themselves probably when they go, like losing a half step in basketball when your ankle is a little stiff. Thought is about something and you pay mind to what it is about, not how quick and right it came.

Momma soon showed me some stuff, though. She saw into me even though I did not even know I was hiding anything, and made me sit down one night and talk about school and then we got around to Home Ec and before I knew it I was telling her all about Bix, or at least everything in Home Ec. I did not tell her about seeing him play shortstop and him being the same and not the same. Home Ec was enough. I was telling her and I hardly knew but I was all of a sudden all full of crying. It was something sad, I didn't know.

She hugged me, the first time she did that since coming home. It made me cry worse. I busted all up. She let me go on and bawl, which what else could she do? It was over pretty fast, and then I was okay and felt even a little weird because it hit so sudden and left so sudden and I did not see it coming or see where it went. Momma did not say anything about it. Instead she said, Tell me, have you been shooting around like you do?

I told her no. She asked how long since I had been playing basketball every day. I told her a few weeks.

She nodded and told me to go get Henri and Maurice. When we were all there she asked them if they had been doing their things they liked, Henri being football and Mo the orphans downtown. They both said no, same as me. Momma looked very worried for a minute and we looked at each other like Uh-oh we should not have told. But it was okay. Momma just said, very serious, she appreciated how dedicated we were and how good at our work too. But from now on we had to get in at least an hour a day of what we wanted most to do besides taking care of her. She told Henri, talk to Coach Poindexter and explain and see if he would let Henri back on the team (which he did and Henri even played the last three games and intercepted two passes). Maurice said he could slip back in at the orphan place easy, and in time to prevent most of the kids from falling into the pre-winter despair syndrome that was just around the corner. Me she told to shoot some hoops. Henri said yes, so I would not be such a crab. I had yelled at him that morning for putting ketchup on my cheese eggs, which taste fine by themselves and not under red goo until you cannot tell they might as well be paper mache. Maurice told Henri not to be chiding me, I was simply displaying a post-primary love object deprivation symptom, and Momma told Henri to go put some ketchup on Mo's head. We all laughed, even Mo. There wasn't going to be any pre-winter despair syndrome in this house anymore.

21.

So I started slipping out for some hoops.
But it was not the same as I liked it, the
same as it had been. I could not get out
until after dinner had been made and we
ate, which by that time it was dusk, being
late fall and the days getting shorter. I was
lucky to get out even at dusk and no darker,
because Henri and Maurice let me off any
cleaning up, taking over so I could be free
to scoot out.

I did not have time to go all the way to my
court in the woods, far away across the
marshes. That court was also darker than
others at night, because those evergreens
were still thick in the winter surrounding
the court and blocked out all possible light
until it was black as a hole. I would have
had more time later at night to play and
could have taken the trip across the
marshes and all, but by then everything
was completely dark everywhere.

So I found myself the lightest possible court at the time of day I could play, and where I could be alone. When you have only an hour you do not want to be wasting it shooting at the same basket with clutzes talking and juking and wanting to play Around The World. You want to practice.

The place I found was this old tar half court in the other direction from town, which you find if you walk through the poor part of colored town and suddenly you are out where nobody lives anymore. There are not even any streets, and the only things alive are a few wild dogs but the bouncing ball scares them for some reason, and I was glad of that.

There used to be a school out here and the court was for the school kids, a county school but it burned down years ago. Now there is only the old black busted foundation pieces sticking up out of the ground looking like the rotten teeth of Old Man Earth.

There is never anybody there. Even if everyone knew about the court they would not come. The burnt place is scary and still smells funny and some kids were burned in the fire and probably people think their ghosts are there or hogwash like that. The court is out in the open with nothing for miles it seems, so you get the moonlight clear but the winds too, and it can get pretty cold.

The other thing that probably keeps kids away is the railroad track. The train that comes down from Washington DC to Florida comes right by the side of the court, maybe twenty-five feet away. It really wails when it blows through and makes a draft that sucks your shots off center, but so what? You can wait it out. It is gone in a few seconds.

So this is where I shot. It was not what I wanted, but it was a rim and a chain net and a ball to bounce on the hard tar. Every night I would run upstairs and put on my gray sweat suit which Maurice had brought me from when he went up to have an interview with his college. It was pretty big on me, but I grew and will grow yet. It has a hood and on the back in dark green the words PROPERTY OF BOSTON CELTICS. Then, on the front, like it was hardly worth noticing, there is a small green circle with the number 6 left out so it shows gray through the green. Just a little old 6, no big deal, but of course it is supposed to make people who know think that this is Bill Russell's practice suit, while other kids must be running around in suits belonging to number 38 or 72 or 5. Of course this is just foolishness, there being probably two thousand of these suits with 6 on it, and anyone could never think it was Russell's anyway, he being very large and people like me quite small. All the same, I liked the suit and it was nice of Maurice.

Then I would look in on Momma and say I was off to shoot and act all excited, which I was not that much, on account of that ugly old court. But still it was basketball and I was alone again, my body getting lighter and faster while I ran out of colored town, throwing a couple of fakes at trees to see how I moved off the shift, snapping my wrists and the cold air smelling like you could take a handful and crackle it like sycamore leaves.

My routine was to shoot as long as I could still see the hoop clearly, and then for the last fifteen minutes or so while it was getting darker to practice passes off the run. They way you do this is, you are dribbling and you make your move and draw your man but then instead of firing it up you whip the ball away from the direction you are looking or behind my back or something, to the open man underneath. The way you tell if you made the good pass is if you hit the metal pole holding up the backboard. It makes a good noise PONG if you smack it center, and a little TING if you nick it, which counts too. You can tell your pass was good even when it is dark, and probably it is even better to practice passing in the dark because you will often want to make passes while not looking in a game.

Most kids do not practice passing when they play by themselves, only shoot shoot shoot. Most people do not have any idea what you are doing when you cut loose of the ball while driving with the obvious intention of gunning it up—though that is just the point, looking like you are going to pop but instead you dish it and it's a snowbird for the dude under. A pass is a sharp gift to a shooter.

One day I invented a new pass to practice just before I had to leave. That happens—you do something new out of a sudden feeling and then you see that it could work if you got it down, maybe changed a little motion or put something new in, and this is very exciting. But I had to leave before nailing this new pass technique, and I thought about it all the next day, itching to get back and work it out. So when I got to the court that evening I did not start with shooting, but went straight into my pass.

It was a pass slung off the backhand dribble, and very tricky. I drift off slowly to the left from the top of the key, stutter step, speed up and beat my man left and it is obvious I am going up to slip the five-foot lay-up off the boards just an iota ahead of him catching up. But I slow down at the last minute and let him catch up and then with him in the air I snap the ball backhand to the low post. It's complicated, lots of pieces, and no room for showing off though there are several places where you make your man think you are doing something you will not. I was really working hard at these pieces, going over everything bit by bit, caring more about getting each step right and in tune, often going through the other steps sloppy until I could get to them in turn.

After a while I was getting the pieces together, and getting so I could repeat the whole process, which is a big important point for getting these little genius things under control. I drove stuttered speeded slowed and whipped, and I started nailing that pole PONG TING TING TING, crisp and clean sounding. It was still light out too.

I heard the train coming, but paid no mind, being at that important point of putting it together. I even heard it slowing down and stopping, but did not bother to check it out. The trains did that sometimes. There is a switch yard just on the other side of Wilmington and I guess the men there radio out to this engineer and tell him to take it easy if they are backed up there, and he cuts his speed or even stops and kills a few minutes if he needs to, until they radio him Come on in. Big deal. A train is a train. I kept practicing.

Then this voice, a real teasy colored whine, came wailing out of the train—Hey boy, it said, it works better if you put the ball through the hoop instead of chucking it at the pole.

Then the voice laughed and another voice sounded like a kid laughed with it but a little behind and too loud like a dumb kid that did not get the big funny joke but just went along anyway.

I ignored whoever it was. I was at a big moment, working out my stutter step and slipping the ball from my right across to my left in front, which is when a sharp defender can swipe the sucker without blinking an eye. I had to get it just so quick he would barely see it. I practiced it about five times very fast, just the stutter step switch drib, stutter step switch drib, again again again. The voice came back.

Look here folks, here's a colored can't even dance!

There was a murmur from more people, some chuckling. I finished my series and went through the whole move. My pass missed the post.

Now I had to chase the ball toward the train, so I thought I might as well look up and see who was doing all this jiving. If you ignore somebody too much it is worse than looking at them.

There was a black man in a blue uniform with a stiff blue cap and black bill pushed back off his forehead, leaning out the top half of a window in the train. Those train windows work funny, you can open only the top. This dude was leaning there, his elbows hanging out, hat shoved back, a toothpick wiggling in his lips, very sassy. He looked about twenty I guess, maybe older, hard to tell in a uniform. At the rest of the windows stretching back off to his right were all these white faces looking out at me, all these northern city people sitting there comfy as bugs on a dog, with their mouths closed and little smiles on their faces, on their way down to Florida to get a suntan and suck up some o.j., riding this nice train on a winter's day and getting a little extra entertainment from a little nigger outside and a big nigger inside.

Who cared about them. I'm not shy. They did not seem mean, just sort of foolish sitting there like watching television. But that cocky ticket puncher or whatever he was, the jigaboo with the big-time stripe on his pants and cap with a badge, he was irritating and I had to try hard to make myself ignore his act. I got the ball and went back to the court.

I guess I did not ignore him completely, for I gave up on the passing, which looked kind of silly, and commenced to shoot a bit, which I knew looked better. I popped a few jumpers, showing I knew where the ball should go, then put on a couple of hanging spin moves down the lane and banked in a deuce, flipped a reverse under the boards with the left hand, stuff like that, very cool but quick, feeling pretty pleased with myself.

But this dude was set to strut for the crackers so of course he pretended not to be impressed. He said, Pretty easy to look superbad when you play with yourself.

Some of the crackers tittered when he said play with yourself. I hit a jump hook.

If you cannot play with yourself, I said, you cannot play with other people. Then I missed a double pump from the lane.

You make a better phi-los-o-pher than you do a hoop player, he said. He pretended the word philosopher gave him all kinds of trouble, like poor woolly-headed niggers never had call to use such smart big words and were out of their league. The crackers loved it. They laughed while he acted struck with himself.

I kept shooting, but he did not let me alone. He started doing the most bush thing you can, which is yell Short! or Off left! when somebody lets fly a shot. He hollered and was right a couple of times though wrong the more, but the white folks did not notice his percentage, laughing all along like he was such an expert. So, annoyed and mad at him for being such a coon as much as for messing up my game, I walked over toward the train.

As I came closer his eyes got a little thin and crafty, watching me for tricks, and the white people looked quite alarmed behind their glass like they had never been this close to a wild country jig before and I might just eat them if I got a whiff of how delicious they smelled. The colored ticket puncher's toothpick stopped wiggling when I stopped walking and faced him.

Okay big man, I said. Let's get it.

Then I snapped a chest pass at him hard as I could snap it WHAM! smack against the plate glass window's lower half he was leaning on, right between his hanging elbows. I guess I knew the plate glass would not break but it was crazy to do anyway, so I must have been mad out of the usual control. The window shook terribly and the crackers all jumped back from theirs and said Ooh! But the ticket puncher handled himself better. He hardly moved. He must have wanted to jump back by instinct like anyone would, but he hung in there and looked the tougher for it like I could not faze him. My ball bounced right back to me and I caught it and stuck it on my hip.

You maybe asking for a game? he said quietly, raising his brows and jerking his chin at me.

If that's what will shut you up, I said. He smiled, and the toothpick commenced to jiggle again. You could see he was glad I was the country savage again and him the civilized shine. It burned me up.

As to your in-vie-tation, he said, I am on duty and must regret to say I decline. A man must do his duty.

Sure, I said. Plus there's your pretty sailor suit. A man like you does not want to go getting his pants uncreased.

A couple of the white folks laughed. I was not especially trying to get them on my side or anything, but I was not sorry to get a nod or two.

You're a smart little black Sambo, ain't you? the puncher said.

Yes, I said. So get your bad tiger self out here and let me make some butter, I said.

He looked at me for a second and then snapped his fingers. Immediately this big black kid popped up beside him. The kid was probably fifteen and tall, and he had that fake mean stare that city slicks come up with because they think it is the opposite of looking like soft country folk.

This is Bobo, said the uniform dude. Say hello, Bobo.

Bobo did not say hello.

Bobo, said the dude, is a star forward on the Takoma Park Junior High triple-A metropolitan greater Washington league runner-up champion Blue Devils.

Bobo grunted.

I hope Bobo has a wonderful career, I said. I bet the Celtics are already keeping an eye on him and in case they miss no doubt he can repeat the ninth grade until they catch his act.

The dude said, Bobo can kick butt on the hardwood, can you not, Bobo?

Whip your black ass, boy, said Bobo. He said it too low for all the crackers to hear, like this was real dirty talk just between us dirty colored folk.

Well then commence to whipping, Bobes, I said. What are you waiting for? Got to change into your blue devil costume or something? Come on, let's get it.

Bobo sort of snarled and tried to look like a streetwise alcoholic junkie robber, then started to come over to where the car ended and there was a door, but the ticket punch held him back.

Wait, he said. Just wait a sec. We got to make this more interesting.

I agree, I said. I've been bored stiff for ten minutes.

That ain't what I mean, Sambo. What I mean is, we got to place a little sporting em-pha-sis on this match. He pulled his head back and looked down the length of the car. We got any sporting enthusiasts in here? he yelled with a grin.

Several white men laughed and waved their hands. The dude nodded and made a sign like he would deal with them in a minute.

We got to place some risk and stakes, he said. For the par-ti-ci-pants as well as for the observers. Like, what do you have you want to play for?

Well, of course I had only my ball. So I thought a minute and then said, I have this leather basketball, but I doubt it would be much use to you, seeing as it will not laugh at your very funny lines or respond in any way unless you actually do some work with it.

It was the leather ball Coach Newk lent me. I would not lose if for the world.

The uniform dude snickered. A ball. Country nigger got nothing but a ball to his name. Ain't you got anything else?

I left my hoe back in the watermelon patch, I said. A few white faces laughed, probably because they thought I meant it.

All right, said the big sporting enthusiast, Bobo here will stand you for your ball. He nodded and Bobo and he made to come out.

Hold on, I said. They stopped. I said, What are YOU going to put up?

Bobo shrugged at the big dude like HE sure had nothing, being just a streetwise junkie alcoholic robber who traveled light and needed only his atmosphere. The uniform dude snapped something at him and Bobo shook his head. They argued a little bit. A couple of the white men made comments like Come on, put something up, or Get on with it we got bets to place and such. A few had money bills in their hands.

What about it? I said.

Okay, okay, said the ticket dude. He looked like he was making a tough decision. He frowned and looked at me, up and down, sizing me up, then looked at Bobo. He decided Bobo's eight inches height advantage or so must be good enough, and so he pulled out this shiny complicated looking thing and said, We'll put up this. Then he and Bobo came on out.

When they got out I saw Bobo was bigger than I thought, both taller and fatter. I bounced him the ball to let him warm up. The other dude snatched it away from him and stuck his face close to it with a frown and studied it, like he expected it to be a cardboard cutout of a ball and not a sphere at all. Or to see if it was genuine leather. He even sniffed it.

Okay, I said, let me see your thing.

He said, oh no, no touchee. But he held it up, and I saw that it was a lantern, a beautiful one at that, official railroad issue with a brass plate on it with the name of the railroad and all kinds of tricky looking features, very classy. I said, Okay. He put the lantern down very carefully and bounced the ball to Bobo.

Listen child, he said, pointing into Bobo's face. You best be winning or you won't see Florida out of your swole-up eyes. Then he went back inside the car and while Bobo went ahead and warmed I watched the big dude shuffle up and down the aisle of the car, grinning and acting all jive and shucksy, taking money and making bets with the white folks. I could see that he was taking all bets, which the crackers were betting on me. This surprised me at first, but then I realized they probably did not care about throwing their money away. They were stalled on their way to throw it away in Florida, so why not get in a little practice here?

I watched Bobo a little. He was typical hip city coon, real street meat. City kids think they can learn all they need by watching pro games on television and then acting like they are those guys. They hear all the words to say, know whether to call the ball The Pill this year or The Egg, whether it's cooler to kick yourself in the rear with your feet as you heave your jumpshot or to let your legs hang limp and spread out, very casual. Style, baby. They are so busy watching themselves on TV you can drive right past them while they fool with the fine tuning, and I am afraid that is what happened to old Bobo the blazing Blue Devil. We played make-it-take-it to ten buckets and he did not get his hands on the ball until I had scored seven straight lay-ups. I spun through him, I slipped by him, once I bounced the ball between his legs and dashed around to catch it on the other side of him and took it in for a finger roll while he still had his back to the basket thinking Now where has The Pill got to? He got a rebound once, dribbled out to thirty feet and let fly, kicking himself nicely in the rear but the shot was two feet short and that was it for his offense, as I closed out the game ten-zip. We extended it to twenty buckets and made it alternating possession, but Bobes still could not cut it. He hollered Hey! when I shot and swore horribly when he shot, he hand checked me, he yelled Get glass! when shooting a shot off the boards but none of them went in, perhaps because the backboard was not glass but iron. I slowed down a little, feeling sorry for him and knowing he would catch it from his uncle or whoever the dude was. But then I heard the engine start to stoke and steam, and as I did not want to give that sucker any excuse to short me I went ahead and hit four in a row to win the twenty. During the last few baskets the dude had come right up to courtside, screaming at Bobo to keep a hand in my face or use the bod or back me in or post me low and all this crap, and while Bobo was listening I was flying. I finished him off with one from the top of the key, PISH, just as the train blew its whistle.

That's it, I said.

The white men inside the car had busted into cheers and were stomping up and down and crowing to beat the train whistle. The dude looked back at them over his shoulder and frowned most dismal. I could see one of his pockets was full of money the white men had placed with him. He must have planned on dropping that wad in Miami but now he would have to match it I guess. His hands were clenching and shaking.

Good game, Bobes, I said.

Bobes said nothing once again but started to slink back to the train. The uniform dude gave him a nasty clip on the top of his head with the back of his hand as he walked past and snarled something and Bobo ran onto the train near about crying.

Well, I said to the dude, you have got me about tired now, in case you want to try your own luck double or naught.

He glared like he was one quiver away from shooting me dead if only he had not left his mighty gun back in DC. But then the train tooted and he looked at it and it started to roll the tiniest bit. When he looked back at me his eyes were crafty and thin again and he smiled this tight little smile and said, See you later, jigaboo. Have a good life here in Uncle Tom's Cabinville. Then he picked up the lantern and ran back toward the train, which was beginning to pick up speed.

Hey! I yelled. That lantern is mine! I can use it!

Kiss off, Buckwheats, he said. You be too dumb to get what's yours.

I ran after him but he had a start on me and by now he was pulling even with the door platform and I could see him setting up to jump on from the run, and I would never see him or my lantern again. Bobo was inside the door reaching out to take the lantern or help his jive uncle on board even though he had just got smacked on the head with his back turned, which shows how bright poor Bobes is.

But then Bobo disappeared, jerked back out of the door, and two white men stepped onto the platform and blocked the way. The uniform dude was by now sprinting full speed and so was I, but he was getting tired, and keeping alongside the train going that fast and faster was getting dangerous.

Hey, he said.

Give the kid the pretty flashlight, said one of the men. They were both bald and overweight, wearing white belts and red pants and those shoes that were woven out of straw or something, but they looked like they meant business and were also having fun, which made them look even tougher.

The big-time bookie was panting by now and sweating bad, running almost full speed and barely keeping up with the train. I was gaining a little on him, but not on the train, which began to pull away.

Hey, he screamed. Come on. Let me on.

The kid won the lantern fair and square, one of the white men said. Cough it up.

I work here, the dude said. The men just smiled. You could see they would let him run clear to Florida and love it.

Give it to him, they said.

It's railroad property, he screamed, stumbling a little toward the train and hollering like a girl in fright as he went near the wheels. I ran smoother on the grass beside the gravel track bed.

Not anymore it isn't, the shorter man said. The other one looked at his watch and shrugged like as to say, Amazing you've made it this long, but soon we'll be leaving you behind.

Help! screamed the poor nigger.

Toot toot! said one man. Chugga choo choo! said the other.

The sucker was almost exhausted. His hat suddenly whipped back off his head and flew under the wheels and got mashed but quick, and he turned his ankle and gasped and sweated, and nothing was going quite right anymore was it?

If you're still here when we come back through next week, said one man, we'll bring you an orange.

Choo choo, said the other, making a motion like pulling a whistle, and the whistle actually tooted. The both of them laughed at this, while the sucker was losing ground faster now and me too.

All right! he screamed but his voice cracked and it sounded silly. He looked back at me quick but hateful and in full stride tried to throw the lantern to the ground but he put too much loft on it on account of the motion and I was able to run right under it and catch it without hurting a thing. I looked up as I slowed down, and saw the men helping him aboard plenty fast now and none too gentle. After all, he had all their money and they would rather he did not stay behind, which he was too nasty to recall or perhaps could have driven a harder bargain. Maybe not, though—I think those white men would have made him come across with the lantern no matter what.

I slowed down and finally stopped, hugging the lantern to keep from jostling or dropping it. Then I went back to the court to get my ball, and sat down on it to rest for a minute and look at my new prize.

The lantern was heavy and rich-looking and beautiful. It was enameled, very hard and thick, looking like the finish on Sting Shields's Thunderbird car that he polishes all day Saturday and Sunday and tells how much he paid to have it lacquered up in Raleigh. The glass was thick and had a few bubbles in it but this only made it look like good real glass instead of cheap stuff.

There was a gold plate on it, or maybe brass I suppose. It said CHESAPEAKE AND DELAWARE and then a little lower there was a date, 1911. Man, this thing was fifty years old!

The last thing I studied was the best. It was a sort of folding shield that slipped over the glass globe, either over half or all of it, which I guessed meant you could cover it up and let half the light out or none if you wanted to sneak. That knocked me out.

On the way home I carried my ball in one hand on my hip and in the other the lantern, swinging. It was heavy but not when you held it right, being so balanced that it swung in your hand just as you stepped and you never really felt it at all.

When I got home I showed it to Henry and Maurice and Momma, telling them all the story. Momma said what I was afraid of, that I ought to take it back to the railroad depot and give it up, as I won it without that man having the right to let me have it.

But then Maurice cleared his throat and looked very serious and said he disagreed with Momma. He said that I had competed in moral correctness and good faith not impeached by improper wagers on the part of my opponent's agent, and to deprive me on the basis of another man's deception of his trust would possibly serve to tip my perspective on material versus moral values. Then Mo cleared his throat again and we all sat for a second trying to figure what he said and I blurted out that for once I agreed with him.

He is right, Momma, I said.

You have no idea what he said, she said.

He said I won it fair and square and will get all wrong-headed if you take it away.

She looked at Mo and he tried to look fifty years old and she looked at Henri and he was trying not to laugh, as Mo's big numbers always kill him. Then she looked at me. What do you want with a lantern? she said.

Light, I said. What else?

All right, she said. Heaven help us for receiving stolen property.

I clapped my hands and slapped Maurice five though I had to pull his hand out flat to do it. Henri cleared his throat and congratulated Momma on a Crisis Averted in my childhood.

Now let me get some sleep, said Momma. And Jerome, I do not want to see that light coming out from under your door at night.

Only place anybody's going to see this light is on a little basketball court in the woods, I said. Good night all.

22.

The next night I was all set. Now I could do my homework after dinner and not have to save two hours for it and so have only one for hoops, being able to knock it down in just over one hour and then cut out for the rest of the night until bedtime. Now I could play in the dark, and also had time to get to my main old court.

Before I left, Momma made me come in and show her I could work the lantern all safe and sound. It was a snap, which it should be with a machine that has class. This baby burned even and clean, did not smell hardly at all, and gave off a grand white-yellow light I could not wait to see in the dark.

I slipped through town without lighting it, not wanting to attract any attention especially somebody like Poke Peters or the Panthers, a gang which hangs around the back side of Left Alley sometimes and are not mean though acting it, but just kind of bored and have a way of wrecking your plans if they snag you. I felt like a secret as I stepped through the town, because now the dark was my choice—I had light if I wanted it, but used the shade like some slinky superdude in a comic.

When I got through town and all the way out to the edge of the marsh fields, I stopped beside a rock and bent all down and lit the sucker up with matches from my sweat shirt pouch. Baboom! Man! The light was fine! It burned upwards yellow and clear, and threw my shadow up so you could not see it in the black sky. There was no shadow on the ground, the lantern being low, and this would be good for hoops.

While I carried it across the marsh I thought how weird it must look to the birds and things watching from the woods, one speck of yellow light bopping over at them like mystery. At first I liked this idea. But when I got really closer to the woods I started to not like it so much.

The reason was, the woods felt different that night. I had never been in them this late, when it was really dark. The dark was quiet and deep-looking but complicated, not just black. The path was curvy and always a bush or tree trunk would be in the way of the light and keep it from penetrating. Also, there were things watching me. I did not think if they were animals or birds or creatures of whatever sort, just watchers, and that was enough to know. I was not afraid of them but it made me feel rude, blazing in on them with my big-time flash. So I snapped down the shield over the lantern glass, and phwoom, there I was in the dark with the rest of the things and it was better. I knew my way through the woods by heart so it did not matter.

I clipped along pretty silent in the darkness. I was starting to get excited about hitting the first jumper of my new nighttime season, my fingers aching to arch that baby up at the hoop lit so beautifully from underneath. I was grinning and juking a little, a head fake her and there, when I suddenly heard a sound stopped me cold and still on the spot.

But as soon as I stopped the sound stopped too. I waited to hear it again but did not, so I crept forward again but very careful to be quiet.

It came again. I froze, and caught the end of it before it stopped, so getting to hear it for what it was clear enough.

It was the sound of a basketball bouncing three times.

A basketball! But there was no light coming from the court. I was at a place I knew, the last bend in the path before the clearing, where these three sassafras bushes sit. I knew if there was a light I would be able to see it through the last trees, but no, there was nothing.

I decided to get closer and check things out as long as I could stay invisible. So the next time the bouncing started I shot around the bend and up to the big cedar on the lip of the clearing about twenty feet from the court. I hung under the lowest branches and couldn't anybody see me even if they were a cat. My lantern was all dark under its shield.

I looked out at the court and squinted and waited for my eyes to get used to the dark. I hoped I might could pin some shape against the hemlocks on the other side of the clearing but no way. That place was black like the pocket of a coat tucked way back in an old closet.

So I listened, and what I heard was strange enough to keep me under the cedar for a while.

At first it seemed just all mixed up, unorganized, and I thought whoever it was must truly be a nut out there. There were a few bounces, then nothing, then all of a sudden a THWONG which must have been the ball hitting the board, which was steel like a gong. Then bounces again and steps light and quick and nothing for a while after that for a few seconds. Then came the weirdest part, giving me shivers down my neck.

A voice whispered, very faint, and what it whispered was numbers.

Twenty-eight. Forty. Fifty-one. Whispered like you do when you are all alone and just want to mention something to remember. You would never whisper if somebody was there, just remember inside.

I kept listening, getting less spooked as it went along. Finally, I decided what it was was somebody playing something out there and it was not hoops.

This was stranger than when I thought it was just a nut fooling around. Some weird game, making the whole thing more mysterious than I thought I would like. Right away I thought I might take off, slip back through the woods and try to hit the railroad court for half an hour. But that sounded miserable, and I got a little huffed at the idea of being scared off my own private basketball court by somebody not even using it to play the game itself. So I stuck there under the cedar and thought, and listened to the bounces and steps and thwongs and those whispers, sixty-two, sixty-nine, eighty, on and on and the longer I heard the less scary and just plain stupid the person out there seemed in the dark, so finally I decided to pull a little trick of my own.

What I would do was creep out a little further into the clearing, and then snap up the half of the lantern shield facing the court. This would throw light out there and nail whoever it was, while I hung behind the light and they could not see me at all. Once I saw what or who and could ask maybe a question or two I could decide whether to come out or take off. Maybe I would scare them away too, just by chucking some rays at them.

So I snuck out from under the cedar and crawled out into the wet grass. I heard a thwong and located the backboard by the sound. I set myself up at the left edge of the court just up from the corner, with the lantern down and ready. I waited until the steps and bounces got going, and then I flipped up the shield.

ZAP! That thing struck some light, I tell you. For a second I was knocked out by how sharp and bright it was so suddenly, but I snapped back and stared hard at what I had caught in my yellow flash.

There was a boy holding a basketball up at his head so his face was hidden behind it, like the light hurt his eyes and it probably did, or like he did not want to be seen which maybe he did not too. I was going to see that sucker, however. I could wait all night.

He was not dressed for basketball. He had on some old floppy khaki pants and a turtleneck sweater raveling at the sleeves and desert boots. Desert boots on my court! I wondered what he thought he was doing there and also who the poor fool was.

I found out soon enough. He lowered the basketball and peeked out from behind it. Light hair, high forehead, light brown eyes, short nose, wide mouth . . . I dropped by eyes from feature to feature as they came into sight and then all of a sudden my insides twisted, for I pieced it together and saw it was Bix.

For a minute I had one of those feelings you can never expect or remember because you get them very few times, only when something truly surprises you, things you thought were separate hooking up behind your back. When you are a smart kid like me you get so you think nothing can sneak up on you. The things you know about you know everything. The people you know do not meet other people you know without you making it happen yourself. People stay put in the places you know them in. But here was Bix, Braxton Rivers the Third, on my place, holding a basketball, whispering secret numbers.

This was like a trick being played on me by big things. My reaction was, step back, tighten up, make sure of Jerome. Play basic defense until you see all the moves.

That is probably why I did not do what would have been most natural otherwise, jumping out all happy and saying Bix my mainest man! slapping him five and whooping it up and playing a little ball right off. Instead I felt far away from that place I knew so well and far away from him, like knowing I knew him but it was long ago, or I could not quite remember how we felt when we knew each other.

Bix did not seem especially surprised by the light nor curious either. He stood still, holding the ball down at his stomach, staring pretty relaxed into the light. That made me feel even weirder, him being so cool. Was this the dude I touched his blood and we were such brothers back a while?

He said nothing, I said nothing, so while I hung back of the lantern I got the itch to do a little jiving. This I do sometimes when nervous, testing things out with a touch of the goof.

Earthman, I said, what game is this? I faked a deep voice.

His eyes got a little bigger but he did not jump or anything. Who are you? he said. Why do you call me Earthman?

My name is called Boo, I said. And I call you Earthman because this is Earth unless I took a wrong turn out at Mercury and got messed up.

No, he said, this is Earth all right. He said it like he might have been telling me this was Cherry Street.

Good, I said. I hate to make mistakes.

Where . . . are you from? he said, trying to sound polite. I could not tell yet if he was jiving me back. Most people would have laughed or said Come off it man, or yelled Get the heck out here where I can see you, by now. But he was content just standing and chatting.

Saturn, I said.

Oh, he said. The place with the rings.

I could not believe this guy now. The place with the rings! Cool as could be, like saying Florida, oh yes the place with the beaches. I was half wanting to laugh, half getting cranky because he was not doing the right thing with my jiving. So I kept going, wondering how long he could keep up.

Right, I said. My spaceship is over there in the next clearing. We landed here to steal some Earthman games, because my people don't know how to play and so they get kind of crabby on weekends.

Oh, he said. Yes, I can see how that would be a problem.

He stumped me, this Bix. I could not decide if he was acting the dummy better than anybody ever could, or if he actually took it in stride I was just dropped in from outer space here in Wilmington NC. Either way, I kept going as long as I could but starting to want to howl already.

So, I said, this is the game they call basketball?

Yes, he said, well, no, I mean . . . the game . . . but this, this is a basketball. He held his ball out and down toward the level of the light like he thought it was my Saturnman eyeball so I could see it better.

This just about cracked me up and I could not hold it much longer. What game is this, then? I said.

Well, he said, it doesn't really . . . well . . . it's . . . I guess you could call it bounceball. Yes, bounceball. He nodded like making up his mind. Then he looked at the light very sincere and helpful and said, Maybe your people would like it.

Well that was the last I could take. I snorted out really loud and my throat just opened up and before I could stop it I was howling. Just howling like a beagle. It was wild. I have never laughed that hard, it even was more than laughing, cackles and yowls and coughs and hoots, too hard really because all the while I knew somewhere it was not that funny and even weird enough to be sad, but I could not stop. I guess my nerves were peculiar that night too. I just lost control and whooped, falling down on my knees holding my stomach, for it hurt from the heave, and then rolled onto my back in the wet grass finding the cold dew very amusing also. I felt my face roll

into the light and I looked backwards upside down at Bix and saw him peering down
at me like not sure yet I was actually not a
Saturnman. He stared for a second and
then looked disappointed. I closed my eyes
and moaned and laughed but it was starting to hurt too much and I was relieved as
it slacked up.

Jerome, he said. You aren't from Saturn
at all.

I yowled.

You lied to me. You told me lies.

Something in the way he said it, lies,
froze me up quick and I coughed and rolled
over onto my knees and looked at him,
shutting up fast. But he was not upset yet,
not like about the lies and cracker pie. He
looked disgusted, but cooler, tougher.

No, Bix, I said, not really lies.

Yes, he said, Oh yes. You think it's a big
joke, but it really is a lie, all it is. People
think the easiest way to be funny is lying,
and they expect you to laugh at everything
that isn't true.

Oh come on, man, I said. I sat back in the
grass and flipped up the other side of the
lantern shield for the heat. Bix, man, I
never expected anybody to believe that jive.
That's the difference. It's only a lie if you
expect somebody to believe you.

He was shaking his head like a wise expert, very sure. No, Jerome. You got to

always expect somebody to believe you. I believed you.

How could you? I mean . . . Saturn, man! I laughed, but not very deep.

So? he said, angry now, looking away and gesturing with the ball, starting to bounce it very spastic with the palm of his hand but he stopped when he saw me watching. So? What do you do? Only believe things you already know can be true? Oh, sure! He barked a little laugh, then straightened up and stuck his face out all noble. See, Jerome, the honest man does not care if what a person says sounds weird, he just goes ahead and believes him because, see, he has trust that nobody will lie because HE never does. He nodded once, like he had said a lesson right. But I could see he was behind it, or wanted to be.

So I suppose you tell no lies?

NO! he barked.

Never a one?

NO! NEVER! He stared hot and ready at me and I think if I laughed or showed I had a doubt he would have jumped on me and torn my head off right there. His face was red and he stuck it out and I saw his hands shaking a little. He saw me look and he looked down and broke his stance to bounce the ball again a little bit, turning away from me.

Hey, I said, Here, that's not the way you do it. I got up and walked over. Let me show you, come on.

He stopped bouncing and turned back to me. Maybe that's not good enough for your game but it's okay for mine.

Oh yeah, I said. Good old bounceball. I forgot. But I stopped short of laughing because he was still close to getting bad. Instead I said, very sincere, What is this bounceball number, anyway?

You don't really want to know, he said.

Yes I do, I said.

No you don't.

Hey, listen, the honest man believes when I tell him I want to know. So believe, man. It's easier than believing I'm from Saturn!

He stared at me and shrugged. Okay, he said. What you do is start from somewhere inside the bulb and you—

The bulb? What's this bulb stuff?

That, he said, pointing down. The bulb shaped thing painted on the floor.

That's the key, man.

It doesn't look like a key. It looks like a bulb.

Or a keyhole, see. That's why they call it the key. But okay, you shoot from out here—

Right, you start from out here, and you shoot it at that steel thing, the fanboard—

That's the backboard, Bix.

Well, it's fan shaped isn't it? And you try not to get it into the circle because it's supposed to bounce off and you run to where you hear it hit and catch it but subtract three points for every bounce and five if it goes in the circle—

No no no, man, dig, you shoot it AT the circle, at the hoop, the basket, the hole, baby. Maybe you shoot it OFF the board first, but the point is to get it in. . . .

He stomped his foot. I stopped. I had not seen anybody stomp their foot older than three. Bix was mad and could barely talk. I watched him for a second while he tried to get cool and talk very patiently.

Listen, he said. His voice quivered but he pretended it didn't. Do you want to know or not, about bounceball? Do you? He was red now, very close to being desperate again, so I felt horrible and said Yes, man, sure, I'm sorry, it's just—

Look. Look, he said, maybe that's what these things are called in your game but I don't know your game and I got no pals to teach me your game like you do and no time to play with people, nice kids like you who play together when it's light out and you can play the game only with teams, with buddies. Okay? I play THIS game, with the bulb and the fanboard and the circle and this old peely ball my stepfather lent me, not even gave, five years ago and you know why?

He waited so I said Why?

Because he wanted me to be a man and baseball was not a man's sport, oh no sir, baseball is for sissies and if I could not be a football player at least I could do basketball. Such a big hero game, he played it when he was a kid and he was a star, whoopee, with this very ball in his high school state championship so he hoped using it would rub off on me and I could be a big strong hero too and grow up to be a big man who marries somebody else's mother.

He was really cranked up and rolling it out, but still in control although mad as fire. Very softly I said, I saw you play baseball. You were the greatest.

Well you won't see me play baseball anymore.

He was glaring around looking everywhere but me. No sir, he said, now it's just good old bounceball for Braxton, with funny names for the things and all. Listen, he said, suddenly turning at me and pointing, looking me in the eyes so hard I wanted to start looking around now. Listen kid, do you know what's so great about bounceball? Know why it's bounceball for Bix?

No, I said.

You play it in the dark and you play it alone. That's it.

He steamed for a second. I said, I play alone a lot too.

Yah, he sneered. You don't have to. You don't have to make up a game that pretends to make a must out of being blind, getting points for chasing a bounce down by ear and silly junk like that. You don't have to be kooky that way. You can get out with some friends and look sharp and wear the right brand of sneakers, you all have the sneakers and the moves, you all know what each other is doing.

But I like playing alone best, even when I can play with people. And anyway, I can't play with people now. I have to play in the dark too, Bix. Only I got a lantern.

He looked over at it like he had not noticed it before. I got it last night, I said. So now I can play again, even by myself.

Why can't you play other times, when there's people? he said. He looked at me all skeptical.

My momma had an accident, I said. She's laid up in bed with her head hurt, and I got to cook the meals.

His eyes went from crafty to sad for a second, and I thought he was on the verge of saying something but he did not get it out. He waited a second more and then said Oh. I'm sorry. I hope she gets okay.

What about you? I said.

He sized me up for a second and opened his mouth. But then all he said was I got to go now, Jerome.

Why can't you play anytime but now, Bix? But he had walked over to my lantern and was bending over looking at it.

This is a good one, he said.

I know, I said. I won it from a guy on the railroad, playing hoops. Basketball.

He looked over at me, very serious and a little shaky. Hey, Jerome, he said. I'll . . . Let's play a game of bounceball for it!

Well, I said, um, man . . . you know . . .

But while I was fretting and stammering and wondering how to get out of this one, he busted out laughing. Hoo boy, he said. Oh wow. You got scared but fast! You didn't dare turn me down in case I got crazy again and you sure did not want to lose this pretty lantern, no sir. Poor Jerome! He laughed on. I chuckled a bit too but mostly out of relief. He had pulled a joke and not a bad one so maybe was more okay than he had looked a while back.

He picked up the lantern.

Can I hold it?

Sure, I said.

He looked at it close up, very studious. He poked here and there like he knew his way around the thing.

Man, he said. Then he held it out at arm's length.

You know what this swivel is for? he said.

No, I said.

He nodded. And then he started very slowly moving his wrist, held out stiff-arm, the lantern swaying back and forth, back and forth, and he swung the wrist faster and the lantern swung fast too, and then after he got up enough speed he started actually whirling the wrist all the way around in a circle though you would think it would break but did not. The lantern all this time started going around smooth as could be, in a big full whizzy circle, making a whole ball of light very large and beautiful and you could have see it for miles. Bix whirled it and made it look easy, but you could see actually it took a lot of control and strength. He had the control, he had the strength, he was using them and he liked it. His face was lit up as much as the lantern inside that big circle of whizzing yellow. He was relaxed, concentrating, yet enjoying all the motion and colors and me being amazed out there just in the dark. On his face you could see this little closed smile, like waiting for a hot grounder in the baseball game, in action, in control. I watched and it was just like it had been during that game when I started to dig him. Only it was better now, because I knew how he had to get back to being like this from all those other ways he got to be in between, weird ways blowing him around, not always smooth and in power like he looked at his best but still he did keep coming back. I felt like I loved him right then, because he swung the light and looked happy so soon after being a mess, and it was my light he was swinging, for me. My eyes squeezed some tears, and I felt warm in the stomach and did not ever want to do anything again to hurt this kid.

After a minute he swung the lantern around slower and slower, never losing control or letting it jerk on the swing. In a few seconds he had it down to half circles and then little moves until finally stopped.

Whoo, I said. Whoo, you can sling that jessie!

He nodded, not really listening, still a little smile. He put the lantern down and looked at it with his forehead wrinkling a bit, very thoughtful.

I let him be. He stared at the light for a minute. Then his forehead went smooth and he laughed.

He looked up at me, and pointed at the lantern. Spin Light, he said. Then he laughed some more. I laughed too. Spin Light, I said. Yeah.

We both sort of chuckled quite a bit on that one. I thought he had just given a name to my lantern, and I liked the name. Spin Light. I called it Spin Light from then on, until this very day, the lantern being the kind of thing so good you can name it like a pet. I was very impressed with him for coming up with such a name.

While I laughed and said it over and over, Yeah, Spin Light, he stopped but kept smiling and nodding and without me really noticing he slipped away and picked up his ball and started to move off.

See you Jerome, he said, cutting across the other side of the court.

Hey, I said, cooling the laugh. Hey, listen—you come here every night?

Yeah, he said, still walking with his back to me, getting further out toward where the light stopped.

Well, how about we meet? How about I meet you here tomorrow? We can, you know, shoot around, play some hoops.

I don't know how, he said, getting to the last fringe of the light and passing out into the dark. He held his hand up for a wave without turning around and disappeared.

Hey, I said. I'll teach you.

Maybe, his voice said back out of the dark. Maybe.

I listened as long as I could hear his footsteps. When they were too far away I hollered out, Hey, I'll bring Spin Light!

He laughed and then I waited but nothing else came so I guess he was gone. I got my ball and the lantern and walked back through the woods. I felt peculiar and great, full of something I knew and something I did not. But I was glad I had him again.

And now it is only since I got his notebook that I know what was so weird and neat and secret and funny about him looking at the lantern like he did, and puzzling at it and then laughing and saying what he said. I could not know back then, I thought it was just a name, but now I see it right here in his book, on the page after Phil Rizzuto talking about the way to play short, here is what Bix wrote at the bottom of the page after covering the whole thing with those words, he wrote:

I WILL PLAY MY GAME BENEATH THE
SPIN LIGHT.

LAST PART

23.

It took six weeks.

We started with dribbling. I could have started him on shooting or jumping or the rules or whatever else, almost so complicated once you think about it all and where to pick your point that nobody with a lick of sense would try to teach somebody basketball. The thing is, you can't do it all at once, no more nor you can just sit down and write a book like this all at once either. You have to go day by day in pieces. So with hoops, which piece do you pick first?

I picked dribbling. I picked it because in basketball dribbling is like walking in any other sport except hockey where they skate. What I mean is, you cannot move in hoops when you got the ball unless you dribble. Now, no baseball coach would try to teach a kid how to drag bunt unless the kid would walk first. So what good of me to tell Bix about jump shots until he could move to the place he wanted to shoot from at all?

Bix truly did not know anything about basketball. His bounceball game also did nothing to get him doing anything with the ball the right way. He bounced wrong, threw it at the hoop wrong, rebounded it wrong, did not know how this ball moved at all because he never saw it in bounceball, only in the dark.

That first night, the one after I found him, he showed up, wearing desert boots and khaki long pants and the old turtleneck sweater. I asked could he do this or that thing, and he just shrugged. I was worried at first he was not really interested but I knew it might just be a state he had to get sparked out of. So I asked him to show me how he dribbled. He said No, why bother? Just show him and he would do it right, why waste time doing it wrong. So I did.

I went through it all pretty quick but detailed. I explained about how you only touch the ball with the fingertips and you dribble from the wrist, not the elbow. I told him how you are supposed to feel like the ball is not really ever out of your hand control, like when it is bouncing on the floor you still have a hold on it, but very light indeed at all times.

He nodded and took the ball and held it in his hands several different ways. He looked at his fingers, how they splayed out, then tightening them up so his palm was not touching the ball anymore. Then he held the ball under one arm and stood there bending his other wrist back and forth and looking at it. All this before putting the ball on the court.

But when he finally did put it down he knew what he was doing. That ball snapped down and back on a string. You can tell by the way the ball spins on the way down compared to the way up, and how hard it hits compared to the arm motion, whether somebody can move it right. Bix could, very soon. I told him he was quick. He shrugged.

Next we started moving with the dribble, walking at first, very slow, always making sure the ball was where we knew it was. Then a couple of nights later we got into crouching, getting low, which you have to do else you want the ball stolen every time. A few nights after that we started picking up speed, moving faster, more sudden. Bix was not in a hurry to learn, though you could see he wanted to pick it up quick as he could, but not move on until he had the thing we were doing. Most people rush and they miss things, but he knew inside him how to make sure every step was right before taking the next. That is how I like it too. We were right for each other that way, teaching and learning.

By the end of the next week Bix was low and darting here and there with three speeds he could shift into and out of all quickly. He could go with both hands, too, for I knew it would be best if he started out doing the left equal with the right. You have to dribble both ways someday. I wish someone had told me when I started, for to ignore the left is easy and you have to come back for it later anyway.

At first when Bix came every night he was all bland and shruggy and not particularly eager. But by now I knew this was just a state he could move out of, and what got him moving was the ball. He was one of those people, you put any ball in their hand and they figure out the best way to use it. He got alert when he touched it and he started to care. Man, he was good so fast. Things grew in him soon as he took them in. He did not just copy you, either, trying to make his body do things your body's way. Instead he got the sense of what you did and figured out how his own motion could make the same sense his way. Bix was not going to be a fake Jerome on the court. He was Bix, and already there were things he did by himself I knew I could not do. They belonged to that shortstop dude. His personality was going to come through whatever kind of ball it was.

His personality maybe, but not those wild moods. Those numbers did not operate on him the way they did in outside places. He still got fierce or cool or even a little crazy but this time it was all only in things he did with the basketball. His moods were turned into pure hoops now. They never blacked out his basic cool either—he concentrated and he was always in control. The spells were like flavors on his whole motion, the way ice cream is always sweet and cold and good beneath the chocolate or maple or even crummy butter brickle.

There was nothing but basketball and him and me inside that flash thrown by Spin Light out in the middle of black above and around, warm enough from our motion and no wind through the trees though it was getting colder and darker as winter came on. We did not really talk at all. We had no words to say so much as motions shown and motions repeated, and I guess we knew how away out there across the dark and through the woods that's all everybody else had, words yakked and words yakked back, television and talk talk talk and more television. We got so we just nodded to each other when we both arrived, and then we moved right into the game. This was not cold or unfriendly though if you asked me long before was that how I wanted to be with my best buddy? I would have said probably not. I would have said it sounded pretty strange, and maybe it was, but it was not bad strange.

Only one time did I get fidgety with the mouth, uncomfortable in all that quiet. We were taking a break after some drills and I sat there thinking the quiet seemed okay but I couldn't figure out WHY it seemed okay, and then this made me start thinking that my liking Bix so much was the same, it seemed okay but when I stopped to think I couldn't figure out why. So I spoke up and said Bix, do you like me enough to be best friends?

He was lying back with his sweat shirt over his face and did not bother to move it, only barked out a laugh and said Jerome please do not turn into a goddam shrink or a female.

What is a shrink, I asked.

It is an asshole that thinks he is a doctor because he can sweet talk people instead of making them well.

I think maybe my brother Mo is aiming to be a shrink, I said, but he is not an asshole.

Then he will be a lousy shrink, said Bix.

I let that pass and we sat on in the quiet for a minute and then I said again, Well, Bix, are we best friends?

He moaned underneath his sweat shirt and waved one of his hands. Look, Jerome, he said. Do I have to ask you if you like your lantern? I have never seen you sit down and look your lantern square in the eye and say Lantern, I am certainly quite fond of you. But do I doubt you like that thing? No. Because I see you spend time with it, I see you pick it up and put it down, I see you USE it. And I can guess without any stupid words that you LOVE that piece of metal and glass. Am I right?

Yes, but—

And here I am every night out on this nowheresville court dinking around with a ball and a hoop but most of all dinking around with YOU. And that doesn't tell you anything about being friends?

Not like words, I said.

Jesus! he shouted, slamming his hand into the ground. What is this huge deal about words? Why would anyone ask such a stupid question as Do you like me? I am out here for hours with you, I believe you when you tell me to spread my fingers for the dribble, I believe you when you tell me to bend at the knees though it feels better bending at the waist, I do everything I hear you say. All this talking crap is stupid stupid stupid, it's for shrinks and females and let me tell you one thing I KNOW, it can drive people CRAZY.

I sat staring across the court at Spin Light. In a minute Bix's voice came from behind me, very clear and soft, and I knew he had sat up and taken his shirt off his face and was looking at me.

Now, he said, do you want to ask how come I know these things, how come I know about shrinks and people going crazy?

Before I could think about it, because normally I would jump to ask just such a question, but this time I said, No. No, I don't need to ask anything, Bix.

And then his arms were around me from behind, very tight, and I did not think or ask anything but only noticed after a minute that he wasn't breathing and then I noticed even more that I wasn't breathing, namely because I couldn't on account of his squeeze, and soon I felt dizzy and was about to bust out of his grip when he let go. I gulped in some air and spun around but he was clean gone.

From that night on we did not talk anymore again, at least not about being buddies and such. As much as basketball was lessons for Bix I thought the quiet was lessons for me, and I came to let myself believe he was right about the way those things happened between us, and I let go of a lot of my questions. Maybe I should have hung onto a few, but it was much easier to believe out there in that light in the clearing in the woods with us moving chest to chest in the middle, that we had things happening between us we did not need to think or talk out. It was trust and curiosity I guess, but mostly it had no name, just digging the way each other could do things, the way your legs could slash or how clever your wrists were, digging yourself as much as you dug the other because you felt him watching and liking everything. Nothing was not noticed. Nothing did not count. Lots of people would say this was nothing to come to love a person over, this silent basketball stuff. You are only supposed to love people over big deals, not just the way he twists with a ball in his hands and watches while you do it a little differently. But I started to think these people were wrong. Anything that could get your heart to where Bix and I were must count as much as anything else. Or at least I thought so then.

In about six weeks Bix had gone from one thing to the next and covered most all I could think of in basketball fundamentals. We went from dribbling to reverses and simple switchovers, all just still dealing with motion and direction, nothing too tricky. Then we studied on angles, which you have to know, cutting the right path to the basket or away from it, getting the drive so your man cannot possibly cover the shot without fouling you bad, staying in position after a reverse so you still have the option of cutting back the way you came and fooling everybody. Such a sense of angles is important, you got to know where you are on the floor and where you can get to if you choose.

After angles we got into shooting, for if you move as well as Bix now you want to pay it off by putting that ball in the hole. First we did lay-ups. Lay-ups were the most natural shot for him to get first, coming off two weeks of nothing but motion. The lay-up makes you connect very clearly how your motion leads to the basket. If you start with jumpers maybe you don't see that every shot you take comes from how you moved before you went up and what position you set up for yourself, but in a lay-up you cannot fail to see this, because you choose your path and you take your body all the way along it, and you get there and you actually almost touch the basket, making the connection all the way. So, lay-ups, left and right, and reverses both ways off the baseline. Then the running hook off the drive, from five and then from eight feet out but no farther because the ball gets too much speed and kicks off the board too hard.

After the running shot the short jump shot, and then through the basic types of jumpers. The fadeaway, the lean. For some reason I did not try the hesitation yet. Bix saw the shots and he did them. He could jump like a monkey and his wrists were good once he was up in the air. He kept control of the ball and forgot about everything but wrist and fingers once the rest of his body did its part to get him clear. That is the hardest thing to do, to concentrate on the last parts to make the shot happen, forgetting the lower body, because people who cannot get to your shot will still have your lower body to get and will kick your legs or shove your waist but by then you have to be alive nowhere but the hands and the eye.

After basic shooting we got into the whole other half of the game which is defense. Now, if you are a good hoops player you figure out right away that you can learn a lot about D just by watching yourself on O. You know your feet and how motion starts and stops on offense. You know the angles a shooter chooses. So, when your job is all of a sudden to stop a shooter and hurt his motion, you can flip things around and you know a lot already. The best player always teaches himself things from his own game, like you turn a neat trick on offense, coming up with a very sharp shot, but even while shooting, in the back of your mind something is thinking This shot could be stopped if the defense man cut later and jumped from the side instead of squared off, or whatever. Only the very smartest hoops player will be this quick and open to flip back and forth so naturally. I do it, always have, and Bix did it too, from the start. He used everything he had learned on O to teach him things on D. So really all I needed to do most of the time was give him plain tips, like Never cross your legs over in a step because then your man can cut back on you and you cannot move without you break your knee, or If you want to block a shot do not jump exactly when the shooter does which you want to do by reaction, but wait and go up half a second later so you peak just after he pauses to pop it, and SMACK you get the sucker clean.

And finally Bix was all set with everything he needed but moves. He had the fundamentals, which is what coaches call them, meaning shooting, dribbling, defense, general head play and basic special techniques like the reach-around steal or behind-the-back dribble. But he still had no moves.

I would have expected him to pick up fakes along with his fundamentals, like throwing the shoulders when he cuts off of the dribble, or double pumping on the short jumper. But he never did these things, he just mastered the motion or the shot, and looked so clean that I never mentioned the fakes. But now that I watched him go through a bunch of motions and shots and dribbles and maneuvers on the court I realized that something was missing and watched and saw he did not put one single move anywhere, not one fake at all, and then I realized too that I could not remember him ever doing it.

Well, I thought, that is funny but I guess I never thought to teach fakes, thinking they just happen naturally which of course they probably do not and I am supposed to teach them too. And probably it is better that Bix has the basic motions down before getting shifty and tricky too, because sometimes kids can fake like a magician but do not put the ball in the hole on account of all their energy is in the trick. So, okay, I guess that's the only thing left and then he can cut loose on his own. I got up.

Hey, man, I said, as he came up straight as a popsicle stick off the reverse dribble and lined a twelve-footer through. Hey, now we got to start the last phase.

Yeah? he said, and grabbed the ball from under the hoop and spun in the air and laid it in from under the other side of the net. Yeah? he said, panting a little and getting the ball again and this time sweeping back for a little left hook that smacked off the board and chingled through the chains. Man, he looked solid, in control.

Now we start learning the best part.

I got some best parts already, Bix said. How about this?

He went hard left but swung the ball between his legs and scooped it up right—and it went. It was a tricky move but it would have been better if he had put a little bit of a fake in there, made like he was going left all the way, hidden the ball more on the move between the legs, hung longer and pumped once before scooping it up. As he did it, it seemed fine, but if he were guarded his man would have not been fooled and maybe made him eat that polite little scoop shot.

Nice move nice move, I said. But not good enough.

No? Then try this, he said, and threw the ball up from about eighteen, high off the board, then charged down the lane, went up and caught the rebound, spun all the way around and flipped it up off the right board and in.

Cute, I said. Would have been better with a head fake before you went up.

I don't need a head fake, he said, hitting a ten-foot jumper left-handed. I don't need fakes at all.

I laughed. But he didn't. He was looking pretty serious. He grabbed the ball a few more times, panted hard and dribbled hard and shot with a grunt and shot again, making them all, driving and gunning it hard hard hard and I saw how in all of this his face got harder too and I knew we were coming up on some trouble.

Finally I cut in and snatched the ball coming through the net and turned and stood with it on my hip. He screeched to a stop and just stood there too, sweating and panting, looking straight at me, no expression really, but eyes clear and wide open and face set but loose, like there was something deadly underneath on his mind and he was determined to keep it cool and light.

He held out his right hand for the ball and raised his eyebrows, like to say Come on, chuck it to me and watch this. But I ignored him, and bounced it a couple of times, looking at him all the while. He gave a little smile and jumped for the ball on the bounce but I grabbed it and swung it behind my back. His smile hung there but it was not a real one and said, What's up, man? Let me shoot.

Fakes, I said. Got to learn some moves.

His smile went and he stared at me back from the panting loose open face. Then he shrugged and spun back at the hoop and went up like he had the ball and then grabbed it as it came through and kept pretending shots and jumping hard and grabbing bounds with a snarl. I just watched. Finally he got tired, and said Whew! making it sound like he was a lot happier than he was, and flopped down on the grass. He leaned way back on his arms and squinted up at me in the lantern light.

No fakes, he said.

Come on, man! What's the big deal? You can't be any kind of a hoops player without fakes! Why are you—

NO, he said, booming it. I stopped and watched him. His eyes were getting bad now. No fakes, no tricks, he said. I don't need them. I won't use them.

Then you won't play basketball for beans, I said.

Yes I will, he said. His eyes got wide again but this time they were hot inside and my stomach tightened up at the weirdness coming on. Oh, I will play all right. I will play better than anybody who DOES use lies.

Oh jeez, I said, smacking the ball down and letting it bounce high over my head, jeez here we are with this lie crap again. Fakes are lies, cracker pies are lies, jokes are lies, everything is a lie to you that is just a move to everybody else. What is your problem, dude?

Never mind my problem, he said. Whatever my problem is, it ain't lying. I do not spend all my time teaching my body to trick people like you do. Part of the game, you tell me. Well, if that's so, this game is not a game at all but pure bullshit. Not for me. If this game is worth playing it is worth playing straight, clean, no cockamamy mumbo jumbo in it. And if it is a good game, then the player who takes it straight will be the best player.

As opposed to whom?

As opposed to any little trickster thinks he is a hot number because he can shimmy and jiggle and wave his arms. You look so damn silly when you do all that crap, and it doesn't DO anything because lies never do.

I threw the ball at him. He caught it and fell back. Come on then, I said. Show me your pure and honest stuff, baby. Let's see if I look so silly tricking your straight white ass all OVER this place.

He stared at me and his eyes were cool and smart again, the hot gone out of them, and he cocked his mouth in a smile like I was showing him things he knew more about than me. Nope, he said. He laughed. Oh no, I won't play you now. I'm pooped and besides I'm still picking it up. I've got to get myself all together on this game and you would tear me up now, but not because of your fancy jigaboo stutter crud. But I'll take you up on it. You just wait a while. I'll whip your butt, Jerome. I'll do it clean, with nothing but drives and jumpers and the straight stuff.

You do the reverse, I said. I suppose that's not a fake?

No, he said. I thought about it and decided it's legitimate. See, you take the ball with you on every motion in the reverse. You don't ever pretend to be doing one thing and then do another. Not like your goofy head fakes and when you wiggle your knees, like that would ever fool anybody. He laughed and shook his head. Oh, you look like such a creep when you do that shit.

Okay, I said. Then I walked over and swatted the ball out of his hands. He stopped laughing and looked up at me. He didn't seem upset, just a little amused and a little cocky, but still there was that secret underneath and I had not got down to it yet.

Okay, I said. Maybe it's about time I released you from having to watch so much sinful lying going down all the time.

Hey, come on . . . He tried to laugh but I cut him off.

Maybe you ought to be free to stick with your truth. I wouldn't want to do anything to flip you out again, you know, make you go crazy and screaming and yelling NO LIES OH NO and picking your hands apart till you bleed, just because you're such an honest kid.

Hey, he said, frowning and getting tight, you better—

Yeah, I better. I better watch it or a head fake might shoot you off to the loony hospital, seeing as you are so sensitive. All right, sucker. You play your straight game, It stays light enough now you can have the court this time of night and practice all you want on your clean motion and honest play. Or who knows? Maybe basketball won't be good enough for you, and you'll go back to that real honest man's game, that true contest of excellence and straightness, that great terrific game of games, bounceball. Hang loose, baby.

And with that I turned and walked off the court over to where Spin Light was standing and picked it up in stride and flipped down the cover over the glass. The whole place went black, and quiet, for Bix did not speak and I did not make any more sound than I had to slipping back into the woods. It was dark and I stumbled a couple of times but I did not lift the cover. For some reason I did not want to leave in the light.

24.

So for about two months I did not see Bix. There was just nothing for us to keep doing. I got to go back to playing earlier in the day, because Momma was better and cooking dinner now, though I kept doing lunches. I went to the court in the woods every afternoon late. I guess if Bix wanted to play his fakeless basketball he could have the nights to himself, like I told him. A couple of times I felt almost like checking, taking Spin Light or even maybe going dark through the marsh and woods, to see if he was out there in the dark by himself doing whatever he thought there was to do. But I didn't.

I was alone again, the way I liked it best. But it felt strange now. First of all, I had got used to being in the dark and not seeing any of the stuff around me, the trees and a couple of hawks and squirrels and such. I had got used to Spin Light too, and sunlight was alive by comparison, and the air felt thicker and like there were more things in it to throw off your shot. That night air and darkness let basketball be the only thing going on. Now I noticed smells and breezes and shadows and they all seemed complicated.

The main thing though was Bix, not being there I mean. I had gotten used to him and used to playing with him without feeling like I wasn't alone. That sounds funny, but it was true—playing with Bix had been as good as alone even though he was all there and I knew it all the time we played. Before Bix, when I was alone it was the way it should be, and nothing was missing. Now, after Bix, I was alone and something WAS missing, no doubt about it.

I had to get back to the game by myself, though. No fakeless ball for Jerome. So I slipped my own moves back on piece by piece like they were old clothes I had left hanging up for a couple of months and did they still fit? They felt all right after I started moving in them, but still something missed.

Once before, a long time ago, I dreamed Bix up as my mystery ghost opponent, all without thinking and I did not even know him back then. I quit and put him out of my head pretty easy. Now I tried to get him back in there. I tried to dream him up again as ghost boy to fall for my fakes but he would not come, I could not hold him up there in the brain. This scared me a little, him getting away so bad, so I forced myself not to think about him and went about my own game with no dreams.

I was in good shape. All that hoops with Bix had kept me on my toes, even though it was what he called straight. I realized now how much I missed my jukes and jives and whips and dips. I had not thrown a mess of wicked fakes in an age.

But now I was hungry for some good old swift deceit, and if the body would be avenged for its servitude to untruth, then I was set to suffer and Egglestobbs and Braxton Rivers the Third could play one on one on my grave, baby. I flat cut aloose. For those two weeks you would not believe your eyes if you saw me, for I never once moved straight, never once went up and shot directly. I never dribbled with one hand only or pivoted the same way twice. I pumped and shuffled. I threw head so nasty my neck felt like it stretched two inches a day. I slung myself through space blind with speed and could not think for cunning, never sure on the way into a shot just exactly how I would shoot it, left hand high arch or maybe switch back to right and scoop it, getting glass or twirling twine, which one? or maybe dishing it at the last second underneath to my main man the pole for the assist of assists. Every time I went up was pure adventure, I was pure mystery to myself and as long as it stayed that way I was the greatest basketball player on the face of the place in space with grace.

Mysterious. I had never been mysterious to me before. I liked it. I always liked other people who surprised me with good stuff because I thought I was smart enough to expect everything before they showed what they had. Now I could like myself the same way. It was like meeting this new dude, invisible, who was made by the moves, and what they made was, he was me. I played harder and harder every night, no stopping me now, cutting through things I never knew could be done, pushing it and forgetting everything else for hours until I would suddenly notice my feet were hot as half-smokes or I would not be able to breathe if I ran to the hoop once more. During that time, all those hours, I was one thing only—the moves. Move and move and move, making me up after every twist and spin, all adding up until the end of the day, when I walked home, I felt so great because I was made up of so many fine things. I would walk home and I would feel the sweat still hot and I would begin to recall them as if I had not noticed while they were going on, in snatches. Oh yes, there is that new sidestep spinback, and that is Me. And yes, there is that hanging switch from scoop to push, hitting nothing but bottom, and that is Me too. The moves piled up and combined into each other and every night I was a new set added to the old, complicated but smooth as air.

I took to calling myself the Jayfox again, which is what dudes I used to play with called me when I used to play with more people and had the moves to beat. Hey, the Jayfox can fly, the Jayfox can sneak, they said, here come the Jayfox and havoc he wreak. I even signed it to a spelling test at school instead of the usual J. FOXWORTHY and the stuffy old white lady teacher gave me no credit for it, pretending she did not know any Jayfox, and as for me she could find no paper with my name on it, even though the Jayfox got a 100 which was sign enough that it belonged to Jerome. I got an A for the grading period anyway even with the zero. You cannot hurt the Jayfox.

I could have kept up like this forever, I bet, and would have turned pro by fifteen if I wanted or gone to Carolina on scholarship and whipped up on Duke and Wake Forest. But I got cut off right in stride, for one day just after I had started to get warm out there, about six shots into my moves, I felt somebody watching me and turned around and there was Bix, off standing at the edge of the woods.

I stopped and stared at him. I probably was frowning and looking pretty fierce. I felt mean as a copperhead most of the time on that court, not really bad or angry but pumped up to beat. Bix just looked at me like normal, though, not scared even when I looked like as to bite him if he came near. He sort of smiled and said, Oh, hi Jerome.

What do you want, man? I said.

He shrugged, picked a couple of pine needles off a tree like he'd seen me do and stuck them in his mouth but he stuck the wrong end in and got no pitch, so threw them down after a second and shook his head.

How come you can come here? I said. How come you are so free all of a sudden?

He shrugged. I could not tell just which way he was being, whether the shy wimp or the straight playing shooter or what. If it was the shy wimp, it went a long way back—he had not been him since before we started playing ball.

What's the matter, man? I said.

Nothing, he said. Hey, can I shoot around for a minute?

Sure, I said, though not really wanting him to. My feet were twitching to gyrate, and I knew if he got on the court it would be for some slow shooting. But all the same

I snapped him a two-handed chest pass, maybe a little harder than need be, knocking him back a step right at the corner of the court. I knew he would just go up from where he caught it so I gave it to him there, for it is the toughest spot on the court to shoot from, being behind the backboard which you got to arch it high and come over the board and straight down into the hoop just on the other side. Sure enough Bix went straight up the second he got the ball, and I have to say I was surprised for sure enough too he popped off a shot arched perfect and dropping like bird doo, PIM through the basket.

All of a sudden when it snapped through the net I got sad for I recalled the weeks we played and thought it was gone now and I missed the dude, for he was a good one though screwy on the subject of moves. Somehow, seeing him hit that shot so naturally, it seemed funny he could be apart from me and yet be good even still.

Nice shot, I said.

Sure, he said. He was already not thinking about it. Nobody says Sure when you tell them nice shot.

Whatever he had on his mind he would not talk for a while, so we just shot around. I hung a few of my recent moves, putting on a show, but the shots were not falling and the moves felt funny with him there, shooting his straight up and down jumpers from twelve and hitting them all from anywhere, pure and true as a spelling champion, like there was only one way to put together the parts of a shot the way there is only one way to do the letters in a word and that's how he did every one, j-u-m-p s-h-o-t. Doing my in-the-air-behind-the-back-loopy-loop-under-scoop off the board in the face of his straight stuff made me feel like when you slip and say God dog! in front of a preacher.

Finally we took a break and let the ball roll away and we just stood there, him sticking his hands in his pockets and me on my hips, and just looking at each. It was still chilly enough for the breath to frost a bit.

All right, Bix, I said. What's up?

He looked away, shook his hand in his pocket to make some coins jingle. Then he stopped. You won that lantern in a game, right?

You know I did.

Yeah, he said. Well, I got a game with something to win too. A prize. And I got to win it too.

What kind of a game? You mean basketball? You going to play somebody a game of hoops for a prize? I was pretty amazed at this.

But he was looking away and did not answer me. You know where my dad is? he said. Everything got very quiet all of a sudden.

No, I said. Where?

Dead. Somebody shot him out walking the dog when I was one year old in Washington DC, where we used to live. My momma says it was a mistake, some killers too dumb to get the right man and the next week they killed a guy in the next block. She says they shot the dog too, my dad's dog, and it was dead too, beside him. I never believed her about my dad until she told me about the dog. Somehow makes it seem real, you know?

I'm sorry, Bix.

It's okay, he said. I never saw him, or least I can't remember. Don't you think it's funny how the dog thing works like that?

Yes, I said, it's strange.

He looked at me and then away. This was the first time he ever talked about himself but he did not seem nervous or even very shy. Bet you don't know where my mom is, either, he said.

No, I said. Where is she?

She's alive. She's up in Duke hospital. Know why I have to come out only at night? Because I have chores. I have to cook and clean and wash clothes and do dishes and rake the snake-sap cones off the lawn so they don't kill the grass. Takes me until about eight every night. My stepfather falls asleep in front of the TV then or else I wouldn't get out at all. I get back before the loud movies come on at eleven.

I did not say anything. He just looked around at the trees on the edge of the woods, and watched a little hawk fly over the clearing.

They put these things on her head and shock the shit out of her, he said. I'd have thought that was a pretty good way to go about killing a person.

Who? I said. Your mother?

My mother. They put these things, in the hospital, these electric suckers or something, strap her down and put them on her head and turn on the juice and let her rip. My stepfather would not tell me but I looked it up in the town library. They call it shock treatment. They have to strap the person down, my mother down. Keeps her from breaking all of her bones, thrashing around out of control and her muscles not holding the bones protected like usual on account of the shock running through them. The shock makes a person so they almost fly, it says.

He nodded and looked around, still not nervous, just not particularly wanting to look at me. What's the matter with her, I said, keeping it cool, that they got to do this thing?

He looked at me right in the eyes for the first time and watched me hard. Crazy, he said.

Yeah, I said, it does sound crazy, but what is the—

No, he said, still watching me. No, I mean her. My mom. She's crazy. She went crazy.

What do you mean, crazy? I said, like it was MY momma or something he was talking about. I couldn't help it—hearing that word, which everybody uses like a cartoon, hearing it used straight and accurate was all of a sudden too much and especially nobody uses it for their momma. I was upset for a second and even mad at Bix, saying his mother was crazy like that. But then I went back in my mind and I saw her there at the Seven-Up game, in her black dress, on the sideline where nobody else would think to go, jumping and hollering BIX BIX BIX. And I shivered hard, for I knew Bix was telling the truth and I knew even worse that I had seen it even back then, something about that woman that was pitiful and going wrong, and the adults saw it then too and shook their heads. It made me feel very weird that you could see it in a person headed for trouble like that and yet nothing to stop it even though you knew: crazy.

Bix said nothing. So I said, How . . . how does everybody know for sure she is?

He made a little laugh but not like anything was funny, and jingled his change and looked off into the woods.

Okay, I said, thinking I had maybe better move away, okay, so what is this game you got scheduled?

He looked back at me and there was a moment of liking me very much because I knew enough to move away with my question, and it was like we were back for that second playing ball and lots of silent communication. Well, he said, she is up at Duke, in Durham. They got a big hospital at the college, you know. She's been there since she went crazy five or six months ago, whenever it was we got into that class where they teach you to cook.

All that time in the hospital, getting shocked like that?

I guess. Every Friday in the evening my stepfather comes home from work and gets me and we drive up to Durham and he drops me at my aunt's house, my mother's sister, name of Maysie. Aunt Maysie. She's got six kids. None of them play anything but war, they don't even have a mitt or a bat in the house, can you believe that? I stay there all weekend. On Sunday we all go to church, and they even let the littlest kid wear his favorite gun in a holster! Man, it is embarrassing. Anyway, so then my stepfather, he comes back Sunday evening and picks me up and we take off back here and get in late and then it's school Monday morning as usual. He, my stepfather, he stays with his mother. She lives in Durham, it's where he grew up. But all during the days he sees my mother in Duke.

Oh, I said.

Don't you see it yet? he said, looking at me.

See what? No, I guess I don't.

You must not have listened. I said, I stay at Maysie's all weekend. I don't see my stepfather until Sunday night, when he comes to get me. To drive back to Wilmington.

Well, so? You said he spends all day at the hospital. . . .

Right! Right. HE spends all day at the hospital. My MOTHER spends all day at the hospital. But who do you think NEVER spends any time at the hospital?

I stared at him. You don't mean you never—

He smirked and shook his head.

You have not seen her?

He won't take me.

You have not seen your mother in that many months?

You got it.

But, I mean, man, she is your momma!

Tell me about it.

I mean, you can't keep a dude away from his momma! It must be illegal or something, Bix. Who is he to say you can't see her, not even your daddy! She might need you, she might really want to see you and he, unless—

I stopped dead and looked at Bix. But he had already thought of it and passed it off very cool.

Unless she told him she doesn't want to see me. But it's not like that. She likes me a lot. She wants to see me, you can bank on that. No, it's him. He admits it's his decision. He says she has never ASKED to see me, but, hey, who knows what she can ask for there? Maybe she can't even TALK, man, all buzzed up with electric bullshit. She wants me, though. She always wants me, I know it.

He started walking around a little and I kind of tagged along, scuffing through the grass. It was getting on toward twilight. There was a nighthawk up high going CREE and he tucked and fell and did that thing as he pulled out, going BRGRGRGR with his wings. It always gives me the creeps. When those things fall they look like they are dead for sure and about to hit so hard they will bust into bones and feathers all over, but then at the last second they cup their wings up and catch air BRGRGR and they swoop out of it and back up. I asked Momma once and she said it was either to catch bugs or to show off to the girl nighthawks.

Bix bent over and picked up the ball in the grass. So, have you guessed yet?

Guessed what? I said.

Guessed about the game. About the bet. No.

Oh boy, he said, and raised his eyebrows and blew a big breath out, like WHEW, and then turned back onto the court and bounced the ball a little. Then he looked at the basket, too far away, and threw up a jumper but used too much arm and it clanged off to the right.

Oh boy, he said. Boy, I really went and did it this time, Jerome.

What? What, Bix?

I bet him, my stepfather, I could beat him one on one for the right to see my mother.

I laughed. You be jiving me, Braxton Rivers. . . .

No. I did. I got him into a fight about it, on purpose, like always happens every Sunday when I ask how she is and he says Fine and I say If she is so fine why is she still in the hospital and why can't I see her? and so on, we go round and round. This time I wanted to get him really smoked, so I gave him all this stuff about how he was not even really her real family, and I was, and he had no right to keep us apart and such as that. It worked. He got madder than hell. He almost poked me one, but I made my offer right before he did, right when more than anything in the world he wanted to get me off his back. I said, Okay, let's solve this for once and for all. He said, How the hell do you mean? I said, Okay, I will play you for it, play you a game of your favorite sport, your old sport you were such a whiz at in high school and college, I'll play you a game of basketball and if I win you have to take me to see her, next time we go, and if you win, I will give up, I won't bother you anymore, I won't ask to see her ever again until you decide you want to let me.

And he agreed? He agreed to THAT?

Bix laughed. Whooee, did he ever! He jumped at it. Sure, you are thinking he did not have to. He has nothing to gain, you think. He is already in control. But see, he is all guilty as the devil about keeping me away, and I know it, and I know how to pick at him and make him worse and miserable and yet even then he won't give in but instead wants to clobber me. I think he is just as afraid of what he might do if he got ahold of me as he is about giving in. So he wants this picking over with. Here he gets his chance. It's a sure thing, for him, isn't it? Wasn't he the big star in high school? The snazzy little guard in college? Doesn't his sissy stepson spend all his time playing stupid old baseball, and never touched a basketball in his life? Well, so, he thinks it's a lock. He thinks I am just talking big. But he knows I would stick by my word, so he plans on putting an end to my picking easy as pie.

How does he know you do not play hoops?

When do I have the time? I cook and clean and I am there when he falls asleep in front of that stupid television and I am there when he wakes up and then I go to bed. On weekends I am stuck in the country with a bunch of fat cousins shooting plastic bazooka guns at coke bottles. And, see, once before, a long time ago just after he married my mother, one night I asked him to pitch some to me so I could get my swing going before Little League tryouts and he refused and so I got mad and called him Fatso. He's not really fat but he thinks he is because he used to be such a nice slender athlete. So he laughed very mean and said he could wrap me around his little finger at any sport I choose except he won't even bother with a girly game like baseball. So I said I would not think so high of myself if all I ever was good at was a dumb sport where you bounce this big ball in short pants fifty years ago, and he got madder and me too and my mother had to keep him from braining me. But the last thing I said was, I would never ever ever play that shitty old game in my life and he better never want me ever to shoot around with him when he got lonesome one day for some fun.

So now he thinks all he has to do is hit ten lay-ups and you are done for.

Right. It will be a breeze for him. He probably won't even practice. He was so happy when I challenged him, but he tried to hide it and act like he thought there was really a contest. Frowned and nodded and said, Well, I'm out of shape, but all right. He was solemn and gracious and he let me set a few of my own terms, nodding and agreeing, Sure, fine Braxton.

What kind of terms? I said.

Well, he let me pick the court.

This one?

Bix nodded. Right here.

When? Did he let you pick when?

Tomorrow night at eight o'clock, Bix said, and looked at me.

Tomorrow night, I said. And just how were you planning on seeing on this court at night?

Well, he said, looking straight at me, not nervous or even being brave, just normal and cool, well I hoped we could use some Spin Light.

You count on a lot. I loan Spin Light to no one.

Oh I didn't want to borrow it, he said. I want you to be there. To be here.

To be at the game? For what? You need yourself a cheerleader?

No, he said, I need myself a friend.

And a light.

And, a referee.

A referee! What you talking about, boy?

You have to do it Jerome! he said, reaching his hands out and getting excited. You have to! I mean, I want you, you know, to be here, to watch. That's mostly it. I want you to see, to see how I can win. But we need a ref too. He's bigger than me and he might try to back in on me like you showed me big men often do, and I want to be able to hold position and get the foul if he—

That's not it, I said. You think you can beat him playing your way, don't you? Your way without fakes.

Well, he said, looking down, sure, I mean . . .

And you just want me to see you do it, see I am wrong. Man! You got some nerve!

Really, it's the ref thing too. He won't play the fine points, and I need them, I need the game to be pure, I need all the protections I'm entitled to, it's only right I should be allowed to play honest basketball—

He'll kick your ass, you know.

He stopped and stared at me.

He'll put it to you but good and you won't be able to stop him or do squat on offense with all your straight crapola. He will push you all over the—

You told me a small man can beat a big one anytime one on one because of quickness.

Well, I said, I did but I meant—

He is old and tired and though he probably knows what he is doing with the ball, I am young and pure and will leave him in the dust.

Yeah but—

But what? But what, Jerome? Can I hit the twelve-footer? Here he dribbled two steps and popped it up and PISH it went down. See? Can I block his tired old set shots if I choose? Can I race past him like those hawks up there, zip! If we play the game right, and true, will I whip his butt one two three four five six seven eight nine ten?

Probably not, I said. He knows the game and has one big advantage.

What? Bix laughed. What advantage can he possibly have, unless it is cheating on the rules?

He will fake, I said, and you will not.

Bix's face went flat and cold. Oh, he said. That again.

You are quicker, sure, I said. But look, man, you cannot take advantage of that quick unless you use it to fool him. You cannot turn his size into slowness unless you get him moving in the wrong direction and you in the other. You cannot just race by him because he will be big and crafty enough to get position some of the time too, so you will have to give him some head and shoulder, show him a little ball, drop a stutter—

No, he said, shaking his head and looking down as I jumped around, demonstrating the moves I told him. NO! he yelled, NEVER.

WHY? I yelled back. What is this thing you have?

He looked up at me, very high and clean like when he told me he believed when I said I was from Saturn. Because, he said, if ever there was a game that must be won straight, this is it. This is the game for the truth. This is where truth comes up the winner. I can't expect you to understand.

So MAKE me understand, I said, walking after him for he began to walk away, just turning his back on me. So if I am so dumb, tell me! If I am such a badass sinner, save my poor young self from the nasties of the lying life! Come on, Bix, tell me what is it you got to be so high and pure about the truth for. I have put up with your mystery jive for so long, man, I deserve to know or else I am just too sick of your wonderful pureness to stick with you.

I stopped following him. He said nothing, just kept walking away from me into the woods.

One thing for sure, I said. I am too sick of you to come and bring my light and referee any jiveass one-on-one white-boy clean-head basketball game to visit his crazy mother at Duke University College Hospital! Forget it, jack!

He turned around. I thought I made him mad saying that about his mother and I was sorry but also mad. He was not, though. He just looked back and said, If I win I want you to come to Duke with me too.

Hah! I said. I had the ball, and I turned and chucked up a twenty-footer that did not come close, kicking myself hard in the tail with my heels and leaving my wrist snapped down at the end of my arm in the air, like some ultrajigaboo HORSE player on the rampage. I turned back and Bix was still looking at me.

You'll come, won't you? To Durham?

What for do I want to go to Durham, even if you could beat this dude?

He looked at me, very calm and cool, making me feel all hot and raggedy and even madder. He shrugged and said, I need somebody to go with me, Jerome.

What for, Braxton? To keep you on the truth, to make sure you don't tell no lies to your momma?

As soon as I said it I did not know where those words came from to my mouth, and I was sorry I said them and even though Bix did not move I saw they did something to him and I started to say I was truly sorry and did not know why, but it was too late. He looked at me and just turned away and kept walking, leaving me regret those words there in the grass but not half so much as I regret them now. He went and I stewed and the heat was out of me, I knew I was going to come back for the game tomorrow, going to go to Durham even, and what was scary was, I was sure even if I did I would not be able to help that kid anymore.

25.

The next night came and I did not eat much
dinner, being a little nervous, which I never
am but felt something big and strange
moving out there. After dinner I put on all
black clothes, having no striped shirt for
referees, and got Spin Light and headed for
the marshes.

Bix had showed up at my Homeroom that
morning before the bell all excited and
chattery. He told me he was going to come
separate from his stepfather to the court. I
guess he wanted it to be like warriors fighting a big duel at some high place.

He said he gave his stepfather directions
and told him to find the court on his own,
which I thought would have been mean
even in daytime but was plain cruel for the
night. But Bix liked the idea of the man getting all riled and flustered by losing his
way and stepping in marsh glop and getting bit by the skeeters and such things,
just before the game. I did not think so

highly of this tactic, and even mentioned to Bix that it seemed a little low for a kid supposed to be Mr. Upstanding. He pretended not to hear me, though. He was all fevered up and his eyes were shiny but did not even really see me while he talked. I knew he was going to be peculiar that night.

I got to the woods early. I kept the lantern covered and planned on watching for them from the woods' edge until both were there and then I would come out. I did not want to be there alone with Bix when his stepfather came because that would look bad like in cahoots and I was not. And I did not want to get there just to be alone with this dude I never met.

So I snuck through the forest in the dark again. I was early and sure thought I would be first, but I was wrong. There was a light near the court, I could see from down the path, and when I got close enough it was one of those big-beam spot flashlights like you take camping. It was propped on a pine cone off to the side of the court so it shone up onto the backboard and basket. While I looked a basketball came flying into the light, banged off the rim and bounced left, where out of the dark came this thick arm to pull it back into the dark part of the court. That's all I saw, just the arm.

Bix's stepfather was out there early to practice. He was out there studying the rolls.

The first thing I thought was Look out Braxton. He had thought this dude would take it easy but he was wrong. While I watched him I saw clear that he had come to play. I was impressed—he comes early through the muck and the bugs and he brings enough light to shoot by and he spends half an hour checking out the roll off the rim and backboard, like any good player will do if he can but most guys never think of it. That is what he was doing, studying the rolls. He was shooting high arcs and low, close and far, off the board and off the rim, soft touch and line drive. I saw him only in cuts at first, as he trotted into the light under the hoop to get his rebounds and then scooted back out to shoot again. But then after a while he came and stood under the rim to the right and started putting the ball up off the board and in and then up again and again and on like that for many minutes, standing there not leaving his feet, just using the arms and eye to figure out how the ball hit off different spots, for every toss was a little bit different, took a different path, with a little different spin on it or a higher angle or some such. Man, Bix was dead wrong. This guy was not the type whose game got ruined by a few mosquito bites.

He was not particularly mean looking or anything. He had red hair but his forehead was getting high so you did not get as much hair as I usually like on red heads, finding them the most interesting-looking white people as a rule. He was about 35 I guess, maybe 40, a little heavy but springy all the same. He wore gray sweat pants that were very dirty, so you had to figure he did some kind of working out regularly, maybe handball which a lot of these old dudes play and it seems to keep them from having heart attacks every day I guess. This guy was probably not in too bad of a shape. He had on a faded loose old purple sweat shirt with a stretched neck hole and the sleeves cut off just below the elbow. It had yellow letters on it, ECTC which is what East Carolina used to be. When I saw the sleeves cut off I thought again, Look out Bix boy, this is no fish but a player who wants his wrists free to pop it. He moved like a player, he thought like a player, he even almost dressed like a player, though wearing crummy sneaks from Sears or someplace, brand-new. At least they were high blacks.

After about half an hour Bix came, just in the shadows on the other side of the court from the flashlight. I suppose he came late hoping I would be there with Spin Light blazing and we would be all set up for him to make an entrance. But instead he had to sort of clear his throat to announce he had made the scene, there being no spotlight and he did not have any big line ready for that setup. So he said Harrumm or something, and his stepfather turned around and gave a little wave the way one jock will give another anytime anywhere when they show up on the same court, very casual and natural and nice, no big deal, like this was not the creepy crazy game that it was. I was starting to like this guy.

Bix however did not look at the man. Instead he was squinting out into the dark over around the place I was sitting under a hemlock, peering though he could not see, looking for me.

Um, he said, in this uncertain voice, uh, Jerome?

Who? said the man, looking around very sharply. Who?

Hey, are you out there? said Bix, squinting and looking very dumb indeed.

Where is the light, Braxton? You said you would bring the light. Then the man looked from Bix out to the woods where he was peering at.

Jerome? said Bix. Hey, come on, man.

The man shook his head. I thought it was just us, Braxton. And here behind my back you've arranged a little gang game, huh? Jesus. He turned his head and spat a wad into the dark.

Bix still did not say anything to the man, but was getting nervous looking around the dark. The man looked at him for another long stare, then shook his head and reached over to where he had put a jacket near the flashlight.

I should have known better than to trust you, he said. You always find new ways of disappointing me, kid.

Bix laughed a nasty laugh at him and then went back to looking out in the woods for me. The stepfather stared at him and then after thinking about it said, Maybe we should have a good hard talk instead of playing ball, Bix.

Ha! said Bix again, looking fast over at the man. You NEVER talk to me. You're no good at talking. You talk like SHIT, if you want to know the truth.

Ah, yes, said the man, the truth. Are you forgetting that you aren't so great at talking to certain people either, boy?

But Bix would not look at him again and was getting more and more nervous, running around the edge of the court looking into the dark for me. I knew his talking with his stepfather was over, so I stepped out and flipped up the shields and blew some light into the place. Spin Light made the only big entrance of the night.

Bix blinked and jumped back, but his stepfather took it pretty cool, just looking over a little curious, and then taking off his jacket and going back to shoot some more flatfoot lay-ups.

Bix was trying to see past the light to me, but he was not so nervous now. Jerome? he said. He grinned and snuck a look over at his stepfather who was shooting, then said in a loud voice, Or maybe it's that guy from Saturn, hahaha! sucking his laugh real weird and letting it get away from him, Hahahaha, until his stepfather looked over and was a little worried for a second until Bix stopped.

It's me, I said, and put the light down and stepped out into the yellow circle it threw. I looked at the man and he looked at me. I'm Jerome Foxworthy, I said. I'm a friend of Bix's.

How many more of you are coming? he said. He looked at Bix. How many more?

But Bix was staring at me, Hi Jerome, he said.

Hi Bix.

Gang war, the man said. I should have known better. . . .

I'm not here to play, I said to him, and I am not a gang, and as far as I know nobody else is coming. Bix is here to play one on one, like he told you. He hasn't gone back on anything. I'm just here because it's my lantern and I don't lend it to anybody.

Sure, okay kid, he said, hitting a little left-handed loop shot. So how come you are dressed like Batman or something?

I . . . this is the best I could do for a referee uniform.

He turned around, holding the ball. Referee?

That's what Bix told me.

For THIS game?

Yes, I said. Don't worry, I know the game and I will call it fair.

Forget it, he said, and put up a little push shot that missed but he got the tip. Braxton, he said, grunting as he shot another, if you want to warm up you better get going.

Bix was looking at him now, and said, Jerome is reffing.

You want to warm up or not?

He's reffing.

Look, said the man, slamming the ball onto the court with his hand so it stays there, a classic thing a player does when he is really riled, look. You proposed this game, okay? I agreed to play it. I did not have to and I will probably regret it but there it is, I did what you wanted. All right. You have to learn to take the consequences of your actions like a man, so I am not going to play weak for you tonight. I am going to whale the tar out of you, frankly. But I am no cheat. Though maybe YOU are, and you think your little pal here can hustle me on a few invisible foul calls. Like I said—forget it.

Jerome refs, said Bix, or we don't play.

Suit yourself, the man shrugged, and picked up his jacket again.

Bix looked at him quickly, then away, then back, then away again. And if we don't play, he said, then I take things into my own hands. You know what that means? That means I go to Duke hospital, I don't stay all nice and good boy out at Maysie's. I go to the hospital and tell them I am Mother's son, I tell them she wants to see me and can't because this man who is not my father keeps me out. I tell them how he won't even tell me how she is anymore, always just says Fine, fine, and it has been months now.

Calm down, Braxton, the man said quietly.

And, and you know what happens if they don't let me in, if you get to them first and bribe them or something? Bix was hopping around now, eyes all glinting yellow and looking like a wolf's. You know what I do then? I sneak in. I find a way, I'm no dummy even though you think I am. I get in and I see her, and I tell her everything, how you kept me out, how you hit me, three times in one day, and—

I never hit you. I haven't hit you three times in five years.

You did, said Bix. Oh yes. Two weeks ago Monday.

That was when you threw the ball against the wall over my desk and . . . I just popped you, you cannot go and count each little pop and say I hit you that many times—

Three times, said Bix, in one day. He was gloating.

The man stared at him and shook his head. You are nuts, Braxton. You need help.

Just like my mother? Just like her? Ha! Bix barked. You going to lock ME up in a hospital too and stick electric things in my head and get rid of both of us? He was getting louder but his eyes were actually cooler and I could see he was just pushing this last bit for show. I think his stepfather saw it too but he could not afford to take the chance of being wrong by calling Bix on it.

All right, he said, calm down. But I could see he was angry. Okay. We'll play. Your little buddy here can ref. If the only thing that puts this craziness out of your head is getting your butt beat in basketball, you got it.

I looked at Bix. How are you going to play it?

Um, I don't know, he said. What do you think?

Jesus, said his stepfather, spitting again.

Ten baskets, I said, win by two. Alternating possession after scores. No foul shots—

if you get called for a foul, you give up your next possession. Okay? I said to the man. He nodded. Okay Bix? Bix shrugged.

He can have first outs, said the man. I gave Bix a little bounce pass.

Play it, I said.

Immediately the man dropped into a good defensive crouch, arms out and waving, knees bent, full of spring if Bix tried anything. I saw right then how foolish Bix had been to turn everything so mean. I think before he started pushing it, the dude was actually feeling friendly and a little sorry for Bix, maybe, and might have taken it a little easy on him. But not now. Now Bix had made it all nasty and tight and the guy was ready to put the screws to him. Bix held the ball, flatfooted, looking at his stepfather's waving arms, then looked over at me with this dull expression like he suddenly did not understand anything, and where was he please? While he did that, the man slapped the ball out of his hands perfectly clean, and dribbled for a second outside, giving Bix a chance to pick him up if he wanted, which was actually nice of him, he could have just bolted for the snow-bird. But Bix was not picking anybody or anything up. He was looking at his hands like remembering something about a ball being there a couple of seconds ago and where was it now? His stepfather went on and took it in for a lay-up and brought the ball back.

One—zip, I said.

The man bounced the ball to Bix and went into his crouch again. Bix stared at him, stared at the ball, stared over at me.

Play it, I said. Come on, man. Wake up.

The man probably could have slapped it again but he waited. Bix nodded and sort of shrugged and frowned, like saying, Sure, hey, I remember, I'm tough, I think. Then he bent low and dribbled to the right, straight as could be, but his stepfather blocked the drive with good position and Bix stopped and tried a straight switchover in front, one of those things that looks good when you do it yourself but without any head or foot fake you leave the defensive man right where you usually bounce the ball, and he swipes it which somehow never happens when you are alone. That is what happened now, Bix dribbling it right in front of the dude's hands and he took it clean, turned, and put up a set shot. It missed, but Bix made no move for the rebound and the man grabbed it and put it in.

Two, I said, two—zip.

The man bounced it to Bix again. This time he was more ready, waking up a little each time, putting on this look now that said Hey, I am the purest and the greatest and truth shall prevail. Then he dribbled straight left and went straight up for that pretty jumper but he showed too much ball and did not even twitch it on his way up so his stepfather slashed it right out from between his hands and was off for another lay-up while Bix hung in the air with his hands up but missing a little something usually required for the successful honest jump shot.

Three—zip, I said. Boy is this fun. Come on, Bix, make it a game, man.

Bix was pretty much ready now, but what he was waking up to was not what he had dreamed. It was sad. He was looking stern, he was playing straight, he was doing his motion just right, but he was getting his ass handed to him in a sling. Every time he wrinkled his forehead and stuck out his chin and puffed up his chest like full of every which kind of truth and justice, and every time his stepfather slapped it away or blocked it or deflected it or faked him off balance or beat him for a bound. Bix woke up enough to play a little D, even made a steal once when the dude thought he was asleep enough to let him cross his dribble in front, but I knew that was the last time Bix would get THAT chance. Most times, the simplest fake threw him out of position. Like I said before, you learn about D from playing yourself on O, and Bix never played against his own fakes because he had none.

After ten more minutes the score was 7–2. Bix hit one jumper his stepfather did not go up on, probably because he thought Bix would be spooked for once by NOT having a hand in his face. The other shot was a lame hook Bix threw up in desperation from fifteen feet after stopping his dribble when the man pretended he was taking a swipe at the ball and Bix grabbed it to keep it safe, like a fool. He hooked it like a girl and the dude got a hand on it and was lucky for Bix because it deflected in.

During this time you could see how Bix became more and more hip to what was happening. Up to 5–1 he could not quite grasp the facts. He knitted that forehead and gritted those teeth and you could almost hear him saying to himself, But, but, I am playing honest ball! I MUST be allowed to win! not knowing that just isn't the way it goes. But he started to see. And once he realized, once it hit him at 7–2, there were two ways he could go with it. One, he could get mean and crafty and fight back, start playing a little jive of his own, for he could pull some moves just by nature of his motion if he let himself. Or two, he could give up and slink and feel so sorry for himself, the world's last honest dude beat down by a crooked old deceiver.

I watched, and saw which he was going to take. He was going to do the weak-ass slinky noble bit. He slunk, he sulked for a minute, then he straightened out and sighed and smiled to himself, lips tight, like he alone knew the score in the world. His stepfather threw him a quick first step and Bix did not budge but stood up and crossed his arms as the man dashed by him and scored.

Eight–two, I said. Hold on a minute.

Bix looked over at me. He was not forlorn now, he was standing tall and looking amused and superior. His little smile said one thing: See what a cruddy game you have? See how unjust? Frankly I am above it all. That is exactly what his look said, standing there with his arms crossed.

Bix, you can't pull this. . . .

He's pulled it before, said his stepfather, panting. The dude was tired, had been getting slower every shot, and standing around was not going to anything but stiffen him up. He's pulled it every time something isn't pretty and needs doing, he said, looking at Bix. He's the all-time champ at being too good for ugly business.

He pushed the ball onto Bix's arms. Bix grinned at him and left his arms crossed and the ball just fell.

I'll take possession if he refuses it for ten seconds, the man said. He was close to finished for wind and wanted to get it over with.

Go ahead, said Bix. Go ahead and beat me with your crappy old moves.

Crappy enough for 8–2, said the man and drove for a lay-up from the left side with a nice little hesitation in there.

No bucket, I said. There's time out. We got to solve this right now.

Oh come off it, said the man, slamming the ball and letting it bounce this time. You don't know what you are talking about, kid. This boy has no guts and he never has had any and he is not going to get them now just because you give him a pep talk. He's too smart for pep talks, aren't you, Braxton? I ought to know. I've been giving them to him for five years.

Rah rah, said Bix, go team. When the going gets tough the assholes get going. Rah rah. He was staring at me and grinning.

Jesus, said the man, looking away and waving at Bix like giving up forever. Then he turned back and pointed his finger at Bix and said, You can mock it, son. You can make fun of the tough getting going, you can stick your nose in a book and your hand in a baseball glove once in a while and try to feel like a real boy, but someday YOU'RE going to have to get going, and if you aren't tough then it is bound to hurt a lot worse and laughing won't make it better.

He waited for Bix to say something but Bix just grinned at me, eyes frozen, and the man went over and got his jacket.

I consider this game a forfeit, he said. Any objections to that?

Come on Bix, I said. Jeez, man, think about your momma.

Hey, said the man. I looked over. He put down his coat and the flashlight and walked over to me very serious. Hey, listen to me, kid. I do not ever want to hear you mention that woman, you understand? You do not know who you are talking about and what you are talking about or what you are saying when you mention her, and I won't have it, okay? Okay? He was shaking his big finger in my face like a poker. Understand?

No, said Bix, and we both looked at him for his voice was suddenly very different. He was standing straight and looked funny still, but now his eyes were blazing again.

No, he said. No, he doesn't understand, and I don't understand when you give the same shit to me. What about it? What about when I mention her? You don't like that any better, do you?

Braxton, the man said, this is hardly the place and the company to bring up your—

Why not? Bix said, taking a step towards the man and putting his arms down to his side and leaning his chin out. Why not? She's why we are here. You NEVER think it's the right time to mention her. You NEVER like it when I try to talk about her, or talk TO her, ever since you married her. She is yours alone, isn't she, and you are the only one who knows her, isn't that right? Nobody is allowed to know her but you. You're the big husband, the big old boyfriend before she ran away and married my father in college while you played your little ball at old East Carolina down the road. Man, it burns you up you got to share her with me, and you know what is the worse thing for you to take? I am even closer to her than you are. I came out of her body, man, and that's how close we are.

The stepfather just stared. I could not tell if he was too mad to speak, or just trying to keep control and be the adult who could take Bix's jive and keep cool about it. After a few seconds he smiled. I thought this meant he was going to do the cool adult number, and I was relieved, for it was getting ugly out there. But I was wrong. The smile was just meanness, and when he spoke in a nice cool voice it gave me shivers.

Maybe I'm wrong, he said. Maybe this IS the place and company to bring all this up.

Maybe if you're so proud of yourself we ought to let you show off in front of your pal and hear how it all sounds when someone else is listening.

He stared at Bix but Bix said nothing. Then he nodded at me as if to say You're in on this now, see what YOU think. Then he spoke: So that's how close you are to your mother, huh? Well, it did her a lot of good when she needed to know, didn't it?

Bix's eyes went a little bad but he stood his ground. I . . . I . . . he stammered but could not quite think of what to say so fast.

The man turned his head at me, leaving Bix just gaping there. Did Braxton ever tell you that he does not lie? he said.

This took me by surprise, and I said, Well, actually . . .

Sure he tells you that. He tells everybody. Why, Braxton is the most truthful little soul on earth, aren't you, Bix?

Bix was just frozen. He still looked mad but his cheeks were pale now and the blotch was on his forehead. His stepfather looked at him and then said back to me, No sir, that Bix has never told a lie. Especially not to his mother. Didn't tell her a lie that last night she was here, did you, boy?

Lies are bad, Bix said, frowning, very quick. Lies hurt people.

Oh, do they? I guess you're right. But the truth never hurts, does it? No sir. We

always tell the truth, and if by some chance
the truth hurts somebody then that's just
too bad, we are safe because we just did the
right thing, didn't we. Didn't we, Braxton?

She asked me, said Bix.

Yes, said the man, and you told her,
didn't you? He waited for Bix to answer but
Bix just looked right between us and
frowned without his eyes focused. The man
turned back to me. He was holding his ball,
the ball Bix had played bounceball with,
very easy on his hip. Some of his sweat had
dried on his forehead and it was powdery. It
made him look old but his eyes were really
hopping.

Let me tell you a story, he said to me. I
just watched him. About Bix's momma, he
added.

She's my momma, said Bix, still staring
weird.

Bix's momma was ... she was having
some bad times. A little personal trouble,
we might call it, some doubts about things,
insecurity. You know what that is, insecurity?

I nodded.

It can start getting to a person, making
them pretty ill. Let's say that was happening to Bix's mother. Lots of things start
going bad when somebody gets down like
that. She worries a lot about anything, she
gets very nervous, she can't sleep, roams

around the house in the middle of the night, all kinds of things.

Couldn't give her sleeping pills anymore, could you? said Bix all of a sudden. He sneered. Took too many once, didn't she? Tried to kill herself because she couldn't stand living with you, that's what.

The man glanced at Bix and then just went on. So she's feeling bad, worse than we know, and she gets worse every night, in secret sort of, when everybody else is asleep. She sits and frets and walks and gets all screwed up. Maybe even during the day she is, oh, you know, doing a few funny things, but they aren't so bad that you can tell she feels as bad as she does. Until you see her at night. Then you understand. Braxton got to see her at night first, didn't he? And he understood the truth, didn't he? That's all Braxton ever looks for, isn't it?

She asked, Bix said.

She wandered into Bix's room one night, the man said. Maybe she watches him sleeping for a while. She loves him. She loves to watch him. She worries about him because he's a little strange, a little messed up sometimes, but when he is asleep she likes to look at him and think maybe he will be okay soon. But this time she needs a little something extra, and when Braxton wakes up she decides to ask him for it.

Boy, you just hate it she didn't come to you, Bix said, that just eats you to pieces, doesn't it?

Well, said the man, looking at Bix, it might have worked out better if she had, don't you think?

Bix said nothing. The man went on.

So he wakes up, and he sees her there, and she reaches out to touch him but he is a little spooked, just coming awake and finding her there, and he pulls away.

She was naked, Bix said. Her skin looked all blue because of the moon and she was cold. And she had a knife.

Maybe she had a fever and took her nightie off, okay? Maybe she was making a sandwich down in the kitchen and drifted off to come upstairs and forgot to put the knife down. Who knows? She was acting funny, feeling very bad, okay?

A sandwich, Bix snorted. You're dreaming. But he shivered bad.

So, the stepfather said, looking back at me, so she asks Bix one question. Here she is, obviously upset, very insecure, and she asks him, his mother now, asks her boy, she loves him very much and she asks him, Do you love me? Simple question. Do you love me? Well, not so simple. Not for our truthful Braxton.

She was weird right then, said Bix, shaking worse though he was still sweating, and whining a little now. She was very weird. You would not have liked it, you would not have liked her very much right then, not naked there and cold and with that knife, so weird. . . .

So her Bix sits up and thinks about her question for a few seconds, sitting there in his bed, studying this matter from every angle so to be quite truthful. And then he declares his answer. He gives her the truth, right, Braxton? Just the truth—nothing wrong with that, surely.

You would not have liked her very much right then, said Bix, his teeth chattering and the sweat coming off his nose. Right at that time, you would have not.

And you didn't, did you? So you told her. She said, Do you love me Bix? and you said, No, Mother. He tells his mother he does not love her. But he forgets to explain that he is just being truthful, speaking the truth about that one particular moment. See, he could not be expected to think back one hour to when she tucked him into bed laughing with him, nor think ahead to the morning when he knew she would wake him up all smiles and have breakfast ready, nor any other time in his life. No, for the sake of the truth he had to pin down how it was exactly at that moment. And I guess she was supposed to figure out that a little thing like loving her could change at any moment and maybe if she calmed down and put on her bathrobe and acted nice he might just love her again for a while.

The truth, said Bix, shaking his head, it's just—

So she believed him. Everybody knows Bix does not lie. She was half ready to believe him anyway, feeling very insecure like she did. She nodded and repeated the word he said, No, like she expected it and it was perfectly okay. Then what do you think she did?

You were out in the hall. You could have stopped her.

She took the knife and she stabbed herself in the wrist and the elbow, where the veins are. Then she tried to hold it in the hurt hand and cut the other one but it did not work. So she ran over to the window and stood there for a second, saying No? No? No? and then she put her fist through the window and jerked her arm back and forth over the glass.

No, Bix said, rocking a little, not yelling or upset, just like he was repeating what she had said. No no no.

So I came in and stopped her and Bix was just lying there in bed watching it. He had nothing to fear, see? because all he had done was tell the truth. So now you see why our boy Braxton cannot stand lies. Because all he DOES have now is truth, isn't it?

Truth is his treasure. There is no judgment as long as you stick to the truth.

I looked at Bix. He had stopped shaking sometime during this last speech and he was balanced differently on his feet. His eyes in the lantern light looked like you took a charcoal stick and pushed them back in his head a little, very dark and all the life in them way back behind. But there was definitely life back there. He watched his stepfather closely as the dude put down the ball to go get his jacket and light. He watched him move away like a dog in a yard you cut across, and then he jumped at the ball, scooped it up and snapped a pass that hit his stepfather in the back. The man turned around, surprised.

Check it, said Bix in a tight little voice.

What? said the man.

Check it, said Bix. Play ball.

You're a sick kid, Braxton, the man said.

Then you'll have a good time overpowering me, Bix said. You like to overpower sick people.

The man stared for a second. I could see he was pooped, as much from all the talking he did as from warming up so hard and playing hard in the game, He sighed, and said, Listen Braxton. You are wrong. You think you can make up for everything by seeing her, telling her you love her now. It's too late, kid. Look, I told you, it wasn't all your fault, she was sick anyway, it was just the last straw. But you can't change anything by taking back what you said. You won't do any good. Believe me, you do not want to see her.

Don't tell me what I want, said Bix. PLAY!

The dude sighed and looked hard at Bix. Then he shook his head and took off his jacket slowly and put it down and picked up the ball and walked over. It's funny how when you are tired your clothes hang different and look even silly, for he looked silly now, creaking down into his defensive crouch but not waving his arms anymore, all the muscles stiff on him and his wind gone and his eyes dead. Even so, when Bix dribbled hard to the right all of a sudden the man snapped to and kept with him, scurrying along and watching, getting back into it a little. But then Bix sprang it, and the dude was done for.

The first sign was Bix's breathing. He was breathing very hard like it was him instead of his stepfather who was tired, but it was a different kind of panting, making little noises in his throat, Bix dribbled hard, picking up speed, looking more scared at every step for he knew what he was about to do and so did I and he wondered if it would break him in two and shatter everything to bits and I did too, for he drove hard and the man was with him step for step and then, with a sick howl coming out of his mouth like it hurt so bad, Bix threw him the wickedest pump fake I had ever wished for and the man went flying up and Bix yowled and went up a second later, putting in the lay-up after the first fake of his life and drawing the foul on the way down. I called it. His stepfather nodded and looked at Bix like he was very surprised at the move but Bix was making those noises in his throat and looking more scared at every minute and took the ball for his foul possession. He did not want to slow it down.

Almost as soon as he held the ball in his hands Bix shot his left foot out and lunged on it and the man jumped back to cover his drive but Bix was not driving. Instead he juked right and hung the man standing there while he ran left and with a leap did a nice finger roll that swished.

Eight–four, I said.

His stepfather got the ball and faked right and Bix jumped back like he fell for it, and the man dribbled across in front to the left. Only Bix had not really fallen for it, he just pretended to by leaning back and now he was right there to step up and swipe the ball clean. He spun and drove right himself with the man a step behind, and he went up but hung there and let the dude catch him, pumping once and drawing the swat on the wrist and then scooping it up off the boards on the way down. Eight–five, but not for long, as he got the foul possession at the top of the key, dribbled once to the left, and went up, his stepfather right with him. But this time he hesitated and leaned his arms forward and made contact and put it in the air and it dropped after a couple of bounces, soft touch. I called the foul, the man nodded, and Bix got the ball back. This time he just blew by the man and laid it in. We all knew it was over from then on.

Eight–seven, I said. Play it.

The stepfather took the ball, but he did not want to play it. He was finished. He was drained out, and not just because he had to chase this new Bix on his feet either. There was something else he was chasing in Bix and I was chasing it too and it made you just as empty. For when I watched Bix out there, he was very beautiful with his moves in operation, now doing the only thing he lacked to be the prettiest hoops kid around, but also he was very sad out there, and it looked dark inside. The stepfather and I felt the same thing, I bet: We were both out of the picture and it would be almost impossible to get through enough to stop Bix's moves or to help them. He was playing by himself out on that court.

There was one other thing about Bix playing, and I had to watch and think hard before it came to me. Once he started making that first move, it was like the moves themselves took over and started making HIM. He looked like the move came along and jerked his body into it and he went along, move makes man. Still, he was pretty, and now he blocked a shot, stole the ball, spun a jumper, got fouled.

Eight–up. He blew in for another lay-up and then stole the ball off his stepfather's first dribble and stood there outside, dribbling, waiting until the biggest and best move came for the final bucket, but there was no suspense to the game, it had been all over since he threw that first pump fake. The only thing now was, waiting to see which way he would win, which shape it would take.

It happened, and it was fabulous. He drove straight at the man, backing him up, then climbed right up his face into the air in the lane, hanging until the dude could jump too, then spinning and lofting a soft hook almost looking over his shoulder at the basket. It swished, clean as rain. I whooped despite all the sad stuff, for it was a beauty of a shot and the winner to boot, and now it was over. Bix would see his mother.

His stepfather just stood there panting, watching the ball bounce its way down. But

Bix was already moving out of the light. He had only one thing to say and he said it without turning around.

This Friday we go, he said.

Nobody said anything. The man and I watched him go away into the dark and listened while his steps faded through the grass. The man just panted, hands on his hips slanted, the sweat pants sagging in the back and showing the top of his ass crack.

Do you need help finding your way out? I said.

He shook his head and looked over at me. Did you teach him all that?

No, I said. Not all of it, anyway.

All those black-cat moves, he said. Jesus.

He would not fake with me, I said. When we played, he would not do it. He said fakes were lies.

Then he is one hell of a liar now, isn't he?

I did not answer, just picked up Spin Light. Do you want to go out with me?

Go ahead, he said. I'm going to shoot around with my ball a little.

I shrugged, and moved off with the lantern. At the edge of the woods I turned and looked back. He was still standing with his hands on his hips, looking off the way Bix went. I said, I'm covering the light now, but he just nodded and lifted a hand. I slipped the shields down over the glass and the dark hit like relief. I headed into the woods and started on the path.

I was about twenty feet in when I heard the ball bounce a few times. I turned around and didn't see anything. I walked back to the last bend in the path and looked through the trees but there was no light. The ball bounced again and then silence until BONG and the rim shaking the chain net. Then it repeated, only this time the shot went in, CHING. Then again, another miss. And still no light.

Man, I thought, what is it with darkness and these white men? But I was in the dark too, and I stayed that way until I got home.

26.

There was one more thing to be done in the Bix story, before he got to his mother and I did too. That was, my momma wanted to meet him before she let me go to Durham with him.

Actually she said I could go to Durham with Bix before I even asked her. I had told her about the game and the bet and all. Then, she said, You may go with him. What? I said, not having asked and not even being sure I wanted to go. You may go, she said, and something in the way she said it told me I probably SHOULD want to go. Okay, I said.

But Momma then said if I was going to be Bix's guest for such a trip, then she ought to meet him, and he should maybe be our guest for supper, maybe the night before we left. Did I think this was a good idea?

Well, part of me did, and part not. I still felt so strong and strange for Bix. He truly fascinated me, but it was not like watching the big cats always behind bars at the zoo. I kept thinking I was getting closer to him, like being inside the cage now but still not touching or not making any difference maybe in all of those huge peculiar things in his life. Every time he shifted into one of his creepy ways I waited to get disgusted and click off, send me walking away, but the click never came. I still drew to him even at the same time I was set back and watched like he was a stranger or creature, full of a new surprise. Something there I felt like I knew even when I could not see it, something in him that maybe nobody but me recognized. I had never felt most of the things I watched Bix feel, so it was not that I understood everything, for I didn't. It was not that I knew what was coming for him, or what mysteries were in back of him, for I did not, and even when I saw the mysteries revealed I was still mystified. But I was not clicked off. It was looking more complicated all the time with Bix, but inside me I was trying to tell myself it was really feeling simpler.

Still, I could not hide that I did feel strange about his bad times, when he went peculiar and you never knew where to stand. I was not sure I wanted my brothers and Momma to get a look at this.

But when I thought about it though I saw all of a sudden why Momma's idea was really very good. Bix was in trouble now, bad family trouble, and headed for something in Durham that might be worse. He could probably use a little piece of family goods right now, right before his visit to his momma. Maybe it would buck him up a little, maybe he could keep some of the good feeling with him all the way to the Duke hospital loony room.

The more I thought about it this way, the better I got to feeling about having him come to supper, and I even got excited and wanting to put on a special good time for him. I jabbered to Momma and she said, even better, the two of us, her and me, we could both cook the supper together. This was the best. We would get Bix in for some peace and mellow for an evening, and then we would fill him up with food we made together just for him.

I was jumping all around about it. The next day in school I jumped on over to Bix's Homeroom, to catch him and ask could he come. He did not act pleased or surprised to see me, nor act like anything especially unusual had happened the last time we saw each other, and at first I was surprised how cool he was but he does that and I knew it. I told him we wanted him for supper. He started to say he couldn't, but then he stopped and a smile, not a very nice one, came over his face and he said, Shit, let the sucker get a pizza for himself, meaning his stepfather I guess, and then he said Sure, why not. I told him when to come and how to get there. He said Okay and walked away into his room.

Momma and I planned out a menu. Thursday after school I did the shopping. We would have pear salad (Momma making it), cream hominy (me), snap beans and pot liquor (Momma), and barbecue chicken (me). For dessert, homemade ice cream, Henri cranking because he always looks to do anything around the house that will help make his arm muscles bulge up.

When I came in with the groceries Maurice saw me and followed me into the kitchen. What's all this for? he said, picking up the bottle of beer you got to have for the barbecue sauce, Momma having to write a note to Mr. Peters so he would sell it to me on account of I am just a kid.

We are having a guest for supper tonight, I said. A friend of mine.

His eyebrows went up and he looked interested. A friend of yours? Your age?

Yes.

Hm, he said, picking up the fatback for the beans and hefting it. I wonder, does your friend—well, would you say his home situation is orthodox?

No, I said, before thinking about it, I guess it is really pretty bad.

Then I realized what Maurice was up to and I looked over just in time to see him smiling and rubbing his hands together.

Ah, he said, unorthodox, pretty bad, hmmmm. Perhaps he suffers from a few severe maladjustments, or overcompensatory aggression?

Listen Maurice, I said, you lay off him.

Maybe a touch of deprivation neurosis? What do you say?

I won't have it, I said.

Even a teeny little fear-arrogance complex due to prevailing uncertainty at the source of reinforcement? Come on, Jerome, I get those in kids all the time, I could fix him up with my eyes closed, just a few key questions—

No! You leave this kid alone.

He sighed. You'll regret it, Jerome. You'll be sorry you didn't take advantage of science, I promise. Poor kid, he said, shaking his head like a fifty-year-old doctor, and walking out.

I did not want Mo's jive science. I just wanted a nice home supper, and it looked like that was what we were going to have. I kept getting more excited. I liked the idea of everybody getting to meet Bix and him them, Mo and Henri remembering him from the Seven-Up game as the star, Bix seeing right off they were good dudes and liking them, everybody fine, and best of all

Momma. I wanted Bix to love Momma. I wanted him to see how grand she was and be knocked out and just love her. I thought this would be good. I did not think anything about it might be cruel, flaunting my together momma next to his electric-shock momma crazy in the hospital, I never thought that, and I still don't know if it made any difference, and I never will.

Momma and I worked all afternoon, side by side in the kitchen. We played around a lot but did the jobs too, even having a flour fight which I gave up on account of not wanting to get too whited up because that mess never comes all the way off. After we put the bird in to cook, we sang: In the oven, the mighty oven, the chicken bakes tonight . . . to the tune of The Lion Sleeps, my favorite song, all the way though with new words and very funny, Momma surprising me by knowing the whole tune and even when to stick in the Bawoomawetts. I asked her and she said she used to listen to a lot of radio when in bed while we were at school and once you have heard the Bawoomawetts you cannot forget them.

Henri came in dressed in his official football sweats and did a few push-ups to warm up for the ice cream cranking. I cut the peaches and measured the cream and barely got the sugar in he was in such a hurry to start. He counted at every crank, Hut one Hut two. He is one of those people thinks you got to count exercises or they do not take. Football makes people like that, they all talk in numbers. When he finished he told us it took 430 cranks. Momma thanked him for the crucial info and we laughed while he went up to shower. That is another thing, football players feel they have to shower after anything more sweaty than tying their shoe.

Maurice walked in, very lackadaisy and whistling and looking in the oven and pots, acting very casual indeed like he did not care a bit we were having an unorthodox kid over for supper, which made me a little suspicious. I was right too, for when Momma said I had best bathe also, unless I wanted Bix to think I had put on flour to make him feel at home by pretending to be a white boy myself, Mo jumped and looked at us and said What? What? Is this kid a white boy?

Yes, I said. What about it?

Oh rats! he said, oh daggone rats. He moaned and pulled a note out from his sleeve and crumpled it up but I grabbed it and it had questions on it he probably planned on dropping into the table chat, such as And tell me (name), do you regard yourself as a victim in dealing with adults? and such crapola. I laughed.

What is wrong with him being white? Momma asked.

Mo sighed. Counseling across the color line is notoriously fruitless, due to pre-conditions of mistrust. There goes a great opportunity for some in-house observation, he said, and stomped out. We laughed and I went up to shower too.

When I finished and got dressed, wearing my blue cords and a snappy yellow shirt and my high whites for dress only with the blue laces, I went down just in time to hear the doorbell finish ringing. By the time I got to the door Henri had already opened it and looked out and said, Yeah?

Do not be so rude, Henri, I said, shoving him out of the way. There was Bix on the stoop wearing a tweed jacket too big for him really and a blue shirt and a dark blue tie. He was also holding a basket with a cloth over it. He looked pretty good.

Hello Bix, I said. Come on in.

He nodded and flashed a big smile at Henri and me. It was too big—I had never seen such a smile on him before.

This is Henri, I said.

Hey Bix, said Henri, sticking out his hand flat.

Dig it, said Bix, slapping Henri the five too hard.

Now, dig it is a very stupid thing to say when being introduced. Henri did not notice, but I did, and I thought it was queer. But then Maurice was there and I introduced him and he peered at Bix like to see if there was any chance of busting the color line with a little counseling anyway, and Bix grinned right into his stare and held out his hand and said, What be happening, Maurice my man?

Maurice, who does not know jive talk from bird song, just looked confused and said Fine thank you and shook hands, but I was nearabout flipped. What be happening, Maurice my man? Where did Bix get this jive talking junk? It was ridiculous. I hustled him into the dining room before he got worse, hoping to ask him what he thought he was doing in private but before I could, Momma came into the room. That put a stop to the jive, at least for a while, because when he saw her Bix dropped everything else from his face and just gaped.

She was beautiful. She wore this light blue dress that I like the best, having asked me which dress I wanted her to wear for my friend and I told her that one, and it looked better than I remembered. Also she had combed out her little fuzz of hair and it looked so fine and neat and tight around her head that I never wanted her to let it grow any longer again. Her skin was like it always is, such a nice coffee color with a little bit of milk, set off and made to glow by the light blue dress. Finally, on her ears she wore the silver earrings I gave her for her birthday two years ago, special order out of BIEDERMAN'S B-BALL EXTRAVAGAN- ZA magazine, tiny silver hoops with little bitty chain nets that dangle down, very classy like any other good jewelry but with that little extra meaning.

She smiled at Bix and her eyes were shining bright and you could see she was opened all the way for him, giving him the whole welcome, and you can hardly keep from wanting to kiss her when she looks like that even if you are a stranger I bet. Bix got the message. He just stood there looking blushed and jiveless, trying a little to mumble something cool or chuckle or such, but not being able to pull it off.

Hello Bix, Momma said, welcome to our home.

Heh heh, said Bix, trying to come up with a slick one, red as a strawberry. He tried to put the big smile back on but it would not stick. He would have stood forever probably if he had not remembered the basket on his arm and suddenly looked down at it and then looked relieved to have something to do. He held it out to Momma and said, This is for you, Mrs. Foxworthy. For everybody. For dessert. I made it myself.

Momma looked pleased and peeked under the cloth and said Oh, how lovely. It will go wonderfully with our ice cream. Thank you! I'll just go put it in the oven to keep warm. Why don't you all sit down and begin serving? Bix nodded, and we sat down.

When I showed him where to sit I whispered, Hey man, what the heck is eating you?

Nothing, he said, giving me the smile. Nothing, my man.

And what's all this My Man crap? You never called me that before. But he just laughed and clapped me on the back, which he never did before either. Maurice was watching us carefully so I did not push it and went to my seat. I was at one end of the table and Bix at the other in between Mo and Henri on one side, and Momma on his other.

She came back in and we started.

Now, I had planned the meal thing out in my head. I thought probably Bix would be in one of his quiet moods and I would have to kind of work him out into the socializing thing, talking to him about the food, telling him stuff like the secrets of the barbecue sauce and had he eaten cream hominy before and did he like it? and such matters. Draw him out very gently, being very nice and jokey, Momma and Henri and Maurice going along just as nice and everybody treating him kindly and by the middle of the meal he would be smiling very shy once in a while and making little comments and straightening up his slink and getting to feel better. He would go very easy from the dumps to feeling pretty good, and we would have done it so nice and smooth.

But I never got the chance to even start. I never got to say ary word about the food or anything else. Because as soon as supper got underway, Bix snapped into the most amazing blaze of chatter I ever saw, not chatter really but very like, a kind of slick charming conversation you never would have believed from him or anybody else under thirty years old not born in France and London and New York. Bam, he just slipped into it like flipping the switch, and from the minute he touched the bowl of snap beans he was on, saying the perfect things to everybody, polite and witty and smart, asking very good questions about Henri's and Mo's interests and Momma's recovery and laughing at the right places and looking concerned at the right places, touching Henri or Momma on the arm at the right time to make points or show sympathy, chat chat chat, charm charm charm, full of style and grace and just blowing me away. I sat there and gaped at him down at the other end, everybody down there leaning together and chuckling and talking with him in the middle like a symphony conductor nodding to Henri for a comment and looking at Momma for her to laugh and winking at Mo like he and Mo knew the score on all counts, and even Mo was charmed into thinking here at last was the perfectly adjusted kid of the world. I watched it and just said nothing. It was the most amazing thing Bix had done yet I believe, and the most peculiar. It might have been the most wonderful too if not for one little thing. That thing was, the whole show was one hundred percent total pure jive.

Nothing but. You could see if you watched him close. You saw him laugh but keep his eye on the person laughing with him though THEY were laughing completely and not watching HIM. You noticed how he used the same tone of voice for different sentences and touched people's arm at the same place in the song, like James Brown always falling to his knees so upset when he sings Please, Please Please, so sincere, but the exact same every show. It was not so plain you would have seen it if you were paying attention to the whole conversation and eating and all. But I was not, I was sitting out there checking it out, and I saw it clear as the moon at night: Bix was putting on some moves. They were good moves, no question, they were putting everybody in the air, everybody but me and I just sat there watching. I didn't even eat. If you want to know, the thing made me kind of sick, to tell the truth.

I guess I had caught it at the my man stage, and probably I could have told him to come off it, made him knock it off and come straight and cut the mess, but I had blown it by not setting him straight then. Even in the middle of the meal I wanted to tell him how wrong it was and how rude, it was very rude to put on for people and let them fall for you like that, especially when you did not have to, they were good people and so were you and would have liked each other fine anyway. But it was too late now. I waited too long. Because if I said anything now, it had gone too far and too deep with everyone too involved. Henri and Maurice and Momma were sincere, taking the fakes but giving back for real, and they would have had too many laughs to take back and cancel too much they had felt when they believed his charm. They would have to be shocked and very embarrassed, and Bix too, and could not begin to apologize once it was out, for the whole flow would be broken and nobody would have anything to stand on, feeling like fools every which way.

All of this I just could not bring on. So I sat tight and angry and picked at my food and they all leaned further away and closer together and forgot about me which was for the best because I could not have faked being involved at all.

It could not go on forever, fortunately. After a while dinner had been so over it was silly to pretend it was still going, so there was a break and Bix and Henri popped up to clear the dishes. Bix insisted when Momma said he should stay put and her clear, him making her sit and saying it was the least he could do. I thought for a minute this would be it and we could get through dessert normally once the spell was broken and then he would have to go home and nobody would ever be wise. I was thinking this and hoping for it, when he and Henri came back in carrying the dessert. Henri was carrying the big bowl of ice cream. Bix was carrying a pie.

A pie. A pie with an A pricked in the top crust. Just a plain looking fresh pie, nice and warm. A good old American white-boy apple pie.

It hit me all of a sudden and I sat up straight and looked at him, but he snapped a look over at me very quick, like taking quick stock to see if I would give it away and deciding I would not and then ignoring me again. So I knew he was going through with the big move of the night, and he intended to take it all the way.

Umm, said my momma, and he watched her closely. Umm, she said, I love the smell of cinnamon in an apple pie.

Yeah, said Bix, shooting me a look and then back to her, yes it is good stuff.

What could I do? What I wanted to do was push his face into the pie and knock him all the way to Duke loony ward by myself only pausing long enough to make him apologize for such a slimy trick and bringing nothing but tricks into our home and pulling such needless crapola on my brothers and Momma who would have given him anything. I wanted to kick ass and take names. But of course I could not.

I could not for the same reason as before. The pie thing was so strange everybody would never understand why in the world this weird white boy would pull such a number. I did not want Momma to be hurt by his rudeness and have to wonder why someone would pull such a thing. So I sat there and actually had to hope that the pie would fool everyone so Bix would get out of the evening as smooth as he came in.

Momma was holding the pie knife over the thing. Mmm, she said, I do love homemade apple pie.

Me too, said Henri, but I like it best on my plate.

You can wait your turn, Momma said. It so happens that Bix has asked me to do the honors of tasting the first piece, so there! She stuck her nose up and Mo and Henri laughed and I tied a knot in my napkin.

Bix was changing very fast right now but nobody was watching him, they were all watching the pie and Momma as she cut it. He was watching her too, but all of the charming boy was fast gone from his face and instead while she cut it, while the big move came closer, he started looking excited like in Home Ec almost, but on the other side now.

Hah, he said, unable to hold it back when Momma finally had the piece of pie on her plate. And he stared hot while she lifted a forkful. He nodded, his eyes pretty nuts. Taste it, taste it, he said.

All right, Momma said, you won't have to twist my arm. Eat your hearts out, boys!

She put it in her mouth. Bix watched and made a noise in his throat and twisted his hands in his lap. Mo glanced at him.

Hah, Bix said. Hahaha.

Momma was chewing and saying Mmmm, so Henri grabbed the pie knife and started hacking a couple of slabs and Maurice stuck out his plate and they started to elbow and jive each other Hey! The biggest for me! and such as that, Bix watching them and nodding. But Momma had realized by now. She stared at Bix and her eyes were sadder than I ever saw them in my life. Oh you poor kid, her eyes were saying, why in the world did you have to do this? I did not want to smash him any more after seeing her eyes, I just wanted to cry for him because if I ever made her understand ME that sadly I would not know where to hide. She just watched him urge Henri and Maurice on, as they took second slices, heaping on the peach ice cream and slabbing it away. Bix did not eat any but he cut more for them and laughed with them while they jived each other, getting all the dessert they could take for once because for some reason Momma was not stopping them and they were not about to ask why.

Momma watched Bix, sad and yet still open with love, and she swallowed her bit of pie and just shook her head once, very slight. We just watched, her and me outside it all, both of us knowing and both hoping it would all be over before anybody else found out. Then she looked up at me and her face stayed sad but it was showing me she understood. We just looked at each other while Bix said Yes, haha, and Mo and Henri took more and pretty soon the whole pie was gone, Momma and me just staring at each other understanding together the whole sad time.

Then all of a sudden the whole big show ran out of steam and as Henri and Maurice sighed and groaned and patted their stomachs and pushed up from the table, all of the jive vanished out of Bix and left him sitting there like a banana skin. But Mo and Henri did not notice, feeling grand with so much dessert, slapping him on the shoulder and moving on out of the room to go do something to make the ice cream settle. But Momma and I saw him fall, like a balloon toy you let half the air out of, from the wild laughing snap dude crash into the slinky pale scared kid in two seconds flat. We sat there while Mo and Henri slammed out into the backyard and it got quiet. Bix was not looking at either of us, just staring into the table in front of him, his forehead wrinkled and eyes confused like he almost did not know what was going on here. His color changed, his shoulders slumped, he drooped all over. But his eyes would not go out. He frowned and his eyes kept a little heat in them, like he would not give up trying to figure something out. So he looked hard at the empty pie plate and set his mouth and fought in his mind like there was something important he was about to forget or something. But Momma moved in. She slipped her arm through his and took one of his hands and stood him up very gentle, and he came up with her and his eyes cooled a little. Momma walked him very soft away from the table and he did not look at me until they got to the door. Then he turned around and looked right in my eyes.

I just could not be all noble. I could not tell him it was all cool and everything was fine because we were so bighearted and dig him in spite of his mean nonsense. Instead I looked him right back in the eyes, which were wide open and no defense, ready for something deep. Maybe I could have used the moment better by shooting something helpful into him but I was hurting so I said:

You are too screwed up for words, man.

It hung in the air for a second and he thought about it, staring at me straight, no shakes. He gave one small nod, a corner of his mouth twitched up like something you see teachers do sometimes when you say something they already knew and were waiting for. Then he said:

Which is why I'm such a good buddy for you, isn't it?

Then he turned and walked out of the room and Momma followed. I kept sitting and listened to them go out the front door and heard their steps go down the street in the direction towards his house. After a minute I got up and flicked off the light and went back to sitting and thinking.

I sat there thinking directly about what Bix said. Right away it hit me—sometimes you say a thing and do not think about

what you have really said—Too Screwed Up
For Words. It was a sharp phrase and Bix
was right not to let it just get away, for I
had told it like it was: There really were not
words for Bix when he went off my map,
and maybe that WAS what kept me coming
back to him, maybe I WAS just puzzling all
this time and could not let go, like a math
problem you cannot solve but keep hauling
out your notebook to work at even though
not liking math worth a hoot.

But then a new thought sort of shook
itself in. The thought was, maybe Bix was
not strange beyond words—maybe my
words had just not caught up with Bix.
Instead of him being the big weirdo and me
all cool in the catbird seat, it might be he
was doing things I SHOULD understand
but could not keep up with as long as I sat
pat on my smarts. Maybe I needed to draw
a new map.

While I was sitting there, shivering a bit
for the hawk was out and coming cool in the
window, something happened that you
usually do not notice until it is over. It was
one of those times when your thinking
itself does not come in words anymore like
packages of meaning. Instead the thoughts
pass into you and out and you are left feeling something without ever having seen
the printing. These times are always pretty peculiar to me but also pretty certain,

and so by the time I snapped out of it I was sure of a few new things.

I snapped out because I heard Momma's footsteps coming very faint from far off, so light you didn't know you had really been hearing them until they got louder. I sat in the dark until she had turned the corner and was tapping slowly up the street, the only sound out there. Then I got up and did not turn on a light and climbed up to my room.

Henri was snoring off the Ritz crackers. I climbed into bed and rolled so I could see out the window where the moon made the eaves white above the black hole. I heard the front door open and close. Then I didn't hear anything until the door to my room cricked open and I knew Momma was looking in at me but I gave no sign I was awake. Usually I would roll and wave and she would wave and that would be goodnight, but tonight I kept to myself.

There was one question left in what Bix had said. True, I had decided, he was right about the beyond-words business being the big thing pulling me through our friendship. That much I could see now. But whether or not that made him good for me I was not so sure. That would be something it took a while to work out, and now that I had started on it I did not want to go after it in words, in talk, with Momma or Bix or anybody else.

27.

I waited out on the street for them to pick me up the next afternoon. I was wearing my good gray pants and my blue jacket and a white shirt and a silver tie that has got little blue frogs on it. I don't especially like frogs, but I don't like ties either and so who cares what is on them?

I did not know what kind of car it would be, so every car that slowed down I jumped at it ready to hop in but it wasn't them for quite a while. I guess I was a little nervous, waiting out there so jumpy and ready and going at every car. I had a queer feeling about the whole day. Too many things had happened leading up to it, and instead of fading they seemed like they were sticking around to add up to whatever was going to happen.

Finally they came. It was a huge red and black car but old. The windshield and windows were tinted dark green so you could not see there were people inside, and when the thing came toward me and slowed down I felt like one of those Japs in the horror movies who has just caught the eye of the giant man-eating bug crunching by. I did not feel any better when the back door swung open all of a sudden, slow and heavy like a mouth very sure of itself. I peeked around the door, and there was Bix, sitting alone in the backseat over on the other side. His stepfather was looking over his shoulder and said Hi boy to me but Bix said nothing.

I got in. We pulled away. Nobody spoke. I said, So this is an Oldsmobile. There was a long sort of rope across the back of the front seat and for some reason, nothing else to do, I gave it a couple of tugs. Nice, I said. Thanks, said the man. That was it for talk for a while.

I sat back and looked at Bix. He looked kind of blank but okay, like he looked a lot of the time. He was dressed up too, almost the same as me but his tie was red and his shoes were shinier. In his lap he held his baseball glove.

Okay, I thought. Here we all are with ties on and our shoes shined, and if we're going to act like nothing has happened between us in the past two days it's not up to me to stir it up. This is Bix's big day and I am here because I said I would, but I'm not the one to make things happen anymore. From here on in it's his move.

Suddenly he perked up and looked out the window at a house we were passing and his stepfather said, There's Braxton's house, and I looked too and saw a nice old brick house with a screen porch and carving over the door which I could not tell what it was and then we were past. Bix looked back at it as long as he could, twisting all the way in his seat until we passed over a hill and then he turned back. His face was plain.

We drove on out of town and got on the road that goes north. It is a straight flat road through the sandy plains and off on both sides far back there are scrub woods but nothing else to see. There were no cars but us. There was nothing to look at or do and nothing to say. I flipped open an ashtray. There was an old licorice wrapper in it and I almost pulled it out just so I could read the writing on it to be doing something. But then Bix spoke.

You should have brought something to do, he said, looking at me.

Nobody told me, I said.

He shrugged. I brought my glove. He held it up. I noticed it was tied up with rawhide thongs all around it, very strange indeed.

It's almost spring, he said.

Yeah, I said, staring at the glove all tied up.

It's time to do gloves, he said. Every year, when it gets to this time, you have to get your glove out and fix it up.

What do you mean? I asked, looking at him. He was looking down at his glove.

This is always my favorite day after the winter, he said, every year this is my favorite day. Then very fast for one second his eyes got soft. Then the soft look shrunk back and he was plain and cool again and said, So, want to watch me do my glove?

Better than looking in the ashtrays, I said.

Frankly I did not think it would be much better than that, but it turned out to be one of the best things I ever watched somebody do. What it was was every year when it got cold and baseball was over, Bix stuck a new ball in the pocket of his glove and tied it shut over the ball very tight with rawhide and stuck it away in a plastic bag in the deep freeze. And then every year just before spring he took it out and thawed it and then he had to work on it. The freeze kept the oils in, he told me, but then you had to go through about a hundred steps to condition the whole thing back into playing shape. He proceeded to do every one of these steps exactly and patiently like the glove was a person and him a doctor operating and the glove would die if he did not do it right. Every step he did he told me about it, talking soft and even all in one tone like he was almost talking to himself.

First he untied the thongs and opened the glove up very carefully like he was not sure he would find the ball inside though he put it there himself six months ago but maybe a bird instead and he did not want it getting loose. He told me once he hit his only ball into a creek on the last day of the fall and so instead of a ball he stuck an orange the same size into the glove and tied that in. He didn't used to stick it in the freezer but just in the attic and next spring when he got it he opened it up and the orange had rotted and the whole face of the glove was covered with a blue fuzzy fungus. He said he rubbed some of the fuzz into the leather and thought maybe it improved the flex in that spot.

He handed me the new baseball that spent all winter in the deep freeze inside this glove and I held it. Next he reached down beside him on the floor and pulled out this large cigar box, and then this little leather bag. Inside the cigar box he had about fifteen bottles and tubes and tins of ointments and pastes and oils and soaps, some of the bottles and tins looking very old, one green tin with much paint scratched off given to him by Gil McDougald a few years back, the shortstop for the Yankees when they came through and played the Carolina baseball team an exhibition, and Bix went down to the dugout late in the game and talked glove with him and it was the secret to flex, Bix said. In the leather bag which he opened and pulled out a little hook thing he had all kinds of strange tools I had never seen, scrapers and wooden sticks with blunt ends and such.

Then he was set and he went at it, as I said, talking all the while. I cannot remember any of the details. It all went so quickly from one paste for flex in one part of the glove to a soap and then scrape clean and oil in another and then wax to keep it stiff for shape, and on through mink oil and balsam paste and beeswax and hickory ash ointment, here and there all over for each part of the glove had its special way of moving and had to be treated just right for that particular job.

It could have been very amusing, very fun, and it probably was most years but now it was cut with a serious feeling, being there in the car, rolling down the road to the loony place with a crazy mother at the end, instead of out on a sunny field where the first grass was greening its way up, which is probably where Bix usually did this number. Still, it hit me as funny a few times, such as when he made me smell it to tell it was too stiff and then note the difference after he had rubbed in the softening gunk, and I laughed for the kookiness and yet the fineness of the ceremony. Bix looked at me like I was doing something very odd and the laugh sounded queer in that car and I snapped off fast. After that I was as serious as Bix and made sure not to crack a smile. In a way this was a sad thing, but still it was interesting.

Finally it was finished and Bix put the glove on his hand and took the ball in the other and sat there popping the ball into the glove very hard from very short away, popping it back to his bare hand almost as hard, then back in and out and so on. All this time he studied the action, starting out frowning like he doubted it was ready. But the frown went as he felt it, until finally he was almost smiling, it was okay now for another season, and he stopped and held the ball in the glove and closed it and said, One of my favorite days, every year. It is always the day the things I like start. It's the first day.

And I was right with him, I was sucked right into the hope that things were starting, watching him an artist and a kid at the same time, working his glove and checking it out and full of hope for a new season of nice, straight ground balls. I felt right then that I was the only one remembered all the weird bad stuff that had gone on before, leading up to this point. It was like everyone else had forgot, Bix had his eyes up ahead and he was not going to turn around—it was the day things began, the day you fix your glove up to catch the new balls coming at you, and if bad had pushed you from behind you did not care, for you had made it through.

But I knew deep down that the stuff behind could not just be dropped like it had nothing to do with what was ahead of him. There was just too much, too many strange angles and things left jaggedy open so you did not know they would ever shut right. I looked at Bix and he was pretty and bright. He looked over at me and gave me a smile, like a shy happy kid. My throat choked and I nodded, and he said, Hey, everything will be cool. Then he just looked out his window for a long time, and I just sat there, nothing to do but smell all the oils in the air and try to see how long I could keep them apart until they blended all together, and then I just sat and waited.

After a long time Bix started making little movements and peering up the road. Then he said, You don't know Jeb, do you?

No, I said, I don't believe so.

Jeb's this really good guy, Bix said. He runs this station, you know, gas, and has this little diner there too and we stop there every time. It's just about in the middle of the trip. We stop on the way up and on the way back unless we leave too late Sunday and he's closed. Bix looked up at the back of his stepfather's head like this was a touchy matter Bix did not want to see happen again. His stepfather said nothing, just drove.

He makes really great hot dogs, said Bix. Wait till you taste them.

Braxton . . . said the man, very low, then cleared his throat and said it again, Braxton . . .

I always get two, Bix went on. You can have two if you want. I think today I'll get one with chili and slaw and one with mustard and onions. No, wait! I'll probably get both with chili. You got to get one with chili too, you'll love this guy's chili. Maybe no slaw, though, sometimes I don't like the slaw—

Listen, Braxton—

There's pecan divinity bars too, and pepsi in the old kind of bottle, it tastes better out of the old bottles, Jeb says.

Braxton, I don't think we will be stopping at Jeb's today.

Bix ignored his stepfather. Wait till you meet old Jeb too, what a nice guy. He wears this paper hat, you know, kind of like the old army caps that fold up like an envelope. One time he gave me one. It had LANCE

CRACKERS written on it in blue and red letters and I wore it. Then his face tightened up. One of Maysie's kids out where I stay the weekends got it wet and it fell apart. They take their bath on Friday night, they are always bathing when I get there, running around naked snatching anything you got. He looked up at his stepfather's head.

Braxton, we are not stopping at Jeb's, do you hear? I'm sorry, but we just can't today.

Bix started singing, very loud, Oh, Jeb has the greatest hot dogs, and the greatest gas and stuff. And if you come to see him, he'll even give you stuff. Oh—

Braxton! I don't want you to get wild about this—

Jeb wears paper hats, you see, and if you're ver-y nice . . . He stopped singing when we passed a sign that said GAS THRE MILES. That's Jeb's sign. He left the E off on purpose, he says more people read the sign that way, on account of they see it's wrong and it gets them. Then all of a sudden Bix stopped chattering so happy and smacked the back of the seat very fierce and his face got red and angry and he said WHY?

I don't really want to explain why, Braxton, but we are not stopping and you have to believe me it is best. You just have to trust me sometimes, Bix. You won't listen about the hospital, but at least let me—

WHY! We HAVE to stop at Jeb's! We HAVE to! Bix was smacking the seat every time his voice rose, and getting so mad I thought he was about to smack his step-father, whining and saying WE HAVE TO WE HAVE TO while the man tried to calm him down but it would not work. We came into sight of this little filling station and Bix was bouncing up and down and whining so bad that it was like a tantrum. So the stepfather finally slammed on the brakes at the last minute and we skidded over with a squeal and made it into the station. Bix dropped the tantrum and went back to humming his little Jeb's song, cool as could be. His stepfather was mad though. He stopped the car and turned around and stuck his finger in Bix's face and said, Okay pal, but you remember that I warned you.

Bix ignored him completely, looking happy out the window. I'm bringing my glove, he said. Jeb'll want to see it.

The door of this little diner building opened and a kid about sixteen walked out. That's Jesse, said Bix, he's Jeb's kid. He's dumb as a stick.

We got out of the car and while we did the kid hollered out Fill it like usual? and Bix's stepfather said Yes. The kid, trying to look like he was doing a very difficult and dangerous thing with great smoothness, jerked the gas nozzle out of the pump and slammed it on the side and then jerked the meter handle very hard, because as anybody knows the harder you hit things the more intelligent and skilled you are. I got out and was stretching my arms up over my head when the kid turned around and saw me. His face went like at a horror movie and he squeezed the nozzle trigger and squirted a big line of gas out into the dust.

Sheez, he said, looking like he had never seen a real live black human being before. I finished stretching and walked a few steps behind Bix and his stepfather.

Bix went in the open door first, yellow light in a rectangle and smells of onions and peppers and coffee coming out, then his stepfather and me behind him. The stepfather sort of shuffled down to a crawl once inside and I was right smack against him almost and could not see past but I heard Hey, Mickey Junior! in a rough old voice I guess was Jeb, and Bix giggling. Hey, boss, the voice said and the stepfather said Hello, Jeb. Then he went to hang up his coat off to the left and I got a look at Jeb, standing behind the counter talking to Bix, who was sitting down at the other end and laughing. Jeb was a big dude with square shoulders and a flat chest and stomach underneath his white apron, sleeves rolled up and tan arms with tattoos. I couldn't read the tattoos but I tried. He was gesturing at Bix with one hand and in the other he held his spatula, loose and kind of confident like it was his best companion and he was always ready to flip a burger for a pal.

I was just a few steps inside the door and now I moved and Bix's stepfather shot a glance at me as he sat down, and then Jeb looked back over, and I saw his big flat tan face with blue eyes all crafty and a huge crooked smile but not for long did I see the smile. For when those eyes lit on me the smile cracked down into a scowl but fast, the eyes went narrow and the hand tightened over the spatula and tilted it toward me like it was a sword. Very fast then he jerked his eyes over at Bix's stepfather, who was looking down at the counter and saying, Coffee, Jeb, which Jeb ignored, staring at him and ferocious angry. Bix was bouncing around still happy on a stool away down, babbling about what he wanted on his hot dogs and maybe two with chili no wait one with slaw. . . .

You must be crazy, Jeb said between his teeth to Bix's stepfather.

Just a cup of coffee, Jeb, said the man. Dogs for the boy.

Jeb shook his head, looked over at me, back at the stepfather, then hawked and turned and spat a wad onto his grill. It crackled and sizzled and bounced around making lots of noise and everything else got very quiet, even Bix for a second. Then Bix leaned out over the counter and looked down at me and said, Jerome, Jeb calls me Mickey Junior, know why? Because of Mickey Mantle, see. . . .

I'll wait in the car, I said to the stepfather. I don't want any food from this joint anyway.

You won't wait in any car on my lot, said Jeb. Any car you're in will be moving, faster the better, and you, he said, slamming down the flat of the spatula SMACK on the counter an inch from Bix's stepfather's hand, you'd better be behind the wheel and fast.

Hey Jeb, said Bix, looking a little puzzled, what about those dogs? Hey, look, Jeb, I brought my glove. . . .

Jeb turned and scowled right into Bix's face. I watched the color drain out and Bix go from all pepped up to all of a sudden very scared and not understanding a thing, like he was hit in the stomach and had no idea why. Then Jeb helped him out, by pushing his face up near Bix's and saying, very rough like wanting to get in a fight even though Bix was just a kid, he said, Stick the glove up your ass and ride it out of here, nigger lover.

Bix just gaped. His stepfather slipped off the stool and took his arm, firm but gentle, and pulled him off, Bix holding his glove and stumbling a little and gaping still at Jeb, with the spit sizzling out to a whisper on the grill. They walked past me and out and I made like to follow them but then spun back. Jeb had walked behind the counter down to see us out but now he stopped dead when I turned. He stood there for a second looking almost scared like I was going to rip his guts out for a snack, then narrow and wary, holding his spatula. He pointed it at me and said, Get out, jigaboo.

All you had to do was give him one stupid hot dog and he would have made it okay, I said.

Get out, said Jeb, or I'll shoot your head off.

Uh-oh, I said, nobody told me that spatula was loaded.

Then I went out to the car and we drove away. Nobody said anything. His stepfather did not say Bix, I told you so. I did not say What a cracker bozo Jeb turned out to be, though the thought crossed my mind. Bix did not say any of the strange things that he might have been thinking. After a few miles, I thought somebody should say SOMETHING so I nudged Bix.

Hey, I said. Hey, Bix?

He just stared out the window. Just get me to my mother, he said. He was very tight, talking very soft but tense. He said it again: Just get me to my mother.

Nothing I could add to that.

So we rode for a while all silent. A few miles down the road I started trying a couple of times to get Bix out of it, asking him dumb questions about stuff out in the fields, like did he know what kind of cow that was for it certainly was an interesting one, wasn't it? or did he know why tobacco barns have gaps between the boards. It was crap chat and he knew it and did not even look at me and his stepfather did not say a word either. Knowing if he answered me it would put Bix even more off by himself.

I guess Bix had some heavy thinking to do. Here he had insisted we stop at Jeb's when his stepfather said no, and it had not turned out too nice for anybody, least of all Bix who got the biggest surprise. Now he was on the way to see his mom which he insisted on when his stepfather once again said better not to. Maybe there were more surprises, and maybe he wasn't so sure he was ready for them.

The other thing that the Jeb's business had done was, it took away one more person from Bix, somebody he had thought things were cool with but they were not and now things were over. Jeb was nobody to Bix really, but I was, his stepfather was, his momma was, and going back in time he had messed up things pretty bad with each of us one by one. He was getting another shot at his momma, but the holes behind him were showing. I read a poem once about an army burning bridges it crossed. The look on Bix's face seemed like he was sniffing some pine smoke in the wind.

So we sat in the car and it got dark and no one talked, all the way to Durham and Duke hospital. We parked and walked into the main entrance and not a word. We got inside, and all of a sudden we were surrounded by all kinds of bustle, but not a peep from us three. There were doctors and nurses and people in pajamas and wheelchairs with blankets over their legs so you could not see what the matter was. There were people walking down the halls pulling beside them these iron stands on wheels, and what was on the iron stand was a bottle with liquid in it that was running right at the very moment down a tube and into the person's arm. On top of everything was a stream of announcements clanging over loudspeakers everywhere DR. ABERNATHY REPORT TO INTERNAL SURGERY DR. JOHNSON PLEASE RESPOND CODE SIX and so on. It was very hectic.

But not us, we were not hectic in the least. We were a little troop of gloom, quiet as if we were all on our way back from surgery where they took out our vocal cords and smile muscles. This seemed okay for we were definitely heading in the direction of more gloom, to judge from the changes in the hospital as we walked, through doors and up steps and winding through halls. The halls got smaller and darker every time we turned into a new one, and the steps seemed like they were steeper and emptier too. You got to feeling very far away from all the bustle back in the main part of the hospital. When we finally stopped, in a narrow old hallway with gray walls and flickers in the buzzy ceiling lights, you felt very far indeed, a different country all of a sudden, and you looked back on those old dudes with wheelchairs as quite gay fellows and good company.

In this hall there was one door and a buzzer. Bix's stepfather pushed the buzzer. Bix just looked at the door.

There was a crackle of electricity noise. I jumped four feet, being a little nervous about how they used electricity in this place, but it was just a man's voice coming over a little speaker grate lost in the shadows above the doorway. The voice said something I could not follow but I guess the stepfather did, for he spoke back at it saying he was here to visit his wife. There was a crackle and then nothing for a time. Then on the other side of the door you could hear a lot of locks turning and clacking. It opened inward. A big white man in a light green pair of pajamas but he had shoes on so I guess it was really a uniform motioned us in and we went.

Wait here, Bix's stepfather said to us, as soon as we were inside. It was a sort of hallway but with a big glass window on the right looking directly into the next room. While the stepfather went down the hall with the big white dude, Bix and I stood there. I let my eyes adjust to the dark and then I peeked through the window to check out the action on the other side. I wish I had not looked.

I felt for a second like you do when you are casually watching somebody you don't know in a restaurant and they take off their coat and all of a sudden they are missing one arm. For a few minutes you stare and cannot understand it—where is that arm? There ought to be an arm there, shouldn't there? You check your own and see, yes, two are standard, so what is going on? It is just impossible to adjust, even to something you know exists like one-armed people. You cannot get over how peculiar in the flesh.

That room had crazy people in it. They were doing crazy things. But though I knew there were such people and this was the place to find them, I could not come to understand the things they did as crazy things, the way when that one-arm man opens his wallet and then holds it under his chin while he gets a bill out you think Now why in the world is he holding it under his chin like that? Instead my mind got right in there and tried to take the weird actions for what they were. One lady wearing three or four dresses and two pairs of shoes one inside the other kept picking up things, ashtrays and magazines and such, and trying to wear them, putting them on some part of her body but they all fell off except one empty tissue box that stuck on her elbow. Now, I thought, I wonder why she is so cold? One old dude was looking hard up in the air over his head and grabbing at things that he thought were up there. So I strained by eyes and wondered why in heck I could not see them myself. Another woman was walking around the room and kept looking behind her and motioning like someone was back there and dragging behind, and I wanted whoever it was to keep up too.

There was one young dude in a corner and he got me the most. He was acting like he was listening hard to somebody talking to him only nobody was. But this guy was listening and nodding very polite and fascinated, but with one trouble. He kept realizing he had something important to say and he just could not remember it to save his neck. He frowned and opened his mouth and snapped his fingers and tapped his lips but it would not come. This really sucked me in. I was pressing my nose against the glass and nodding at the dude, like I was the person he was trying to say it to, and I started doing it myself, trying to remember and help him out. I probably would have started, and gone from there to snapping at invisible flies, except this smooth voice came over my shoulder and said:

Well well, little brother, I thought our people had better sense than to bring their crazy selves into a dump like this.

I turned around and there was a young black dude wearing those green pajamas, and patent leather shoes glinting in the dark. He was very bright and smiling very crafty. I would have said something to him but just at that moment, because he broke the spell of watching through the window, I suddenly got the sense of what I had been watching, crazy people doing genuine crazy mess, and I was sort of surprised to see it that way so sudden. I gaped back through the window and watched them grab some air and do some spinning, and it was worse watching when I knew.

The dude watched with me and said, Pretty wild, eh bro? These white folks can sure throw a groovy party! He laughed at that, then said, Do you plan on joining this bunch?

What? Oh, I said, no. I'm not here to be crazy, I'm just visiting.

Ah, he said, I see. Well, in a way for you that's good, but in a way it's too bad. This place will probably be the last joint in the country to get integrated. He laughed again.

What about you? I said. You look like you have integrated it okay.

Oh, touché, brother, he said, watching me closely and sizing me up again, but very amused. Touché. But alas I am not technically OF this place, you see. I do not technically PERTAIN here. Not just because of the skin, dig—because of the threads even more. Anybody you see wearing this kind of funny suit is OUTSIDE all this jive in that room, and they will never get into these people's society OR their heads.

What does that uniform mean?

It means, little man, that I am what is called an ORDERLY. Any black man you see in this hospital is called the same thing, you dig? That is their name for nigger around here. And when you think of it, the name is not such a terrible one in a place where everyone else is either sick or playing bwana. Not bad, eh? Niggers be the secret police in charge of order! He laughed some more, very soft.

Why aren't there any black patients? I said, looking through the window and seeing that the guy in the corner had still not remembered his important message for me.

I told you before, said the black dude. Better sense than to go all the way nuts. Dig, we are half crazy as it is, ALL the time. That's HEALTHY. He laughed and winked, like to show he was proud of being half there himself, and said, The idea of taking it to extremes so you can treat it like malaria, that's the white man's.

I started to say something but I felt Bix move behind me and I spun around. I had forgotten about him for a minute and now he was walking off down the hall behind his stepfather who must have come back. I took a couple of steps, and then turned back to say good-bye to the black orderly. He was gone, vanished, almost like he had not even been there.

I hurried and caught up with Bix and his stepfather at this large doorway leading into a well-lit room. They were waiting on the edge, Bix's stepfather with his back to the room blocking the view in. As I came up he said, Braxton, do you want me to tell her you are coming?

Bix shook his head.

All right, said the stepfather. Then he looked over at me.

I helped him out. Hey Bix, I said, if it's okay with you I will just wait here for you. Okay?

He barely nodded.

His stepfather looked at me gratefully. Then he stooped down and said to Bix, Are you ready? Bix nodded again, barely. All right, said the man, straightening up. I'll just go in first, and you come in just a minute.

Then he turned and walked into the room. We stepped up and stood on the edge of the dark and looked in.

It was one of those long rooms with beds on both walls and a big aisle down the middle passing by the foot of every bed. There were people on or near every bed, all dressed in white smocks. I did not look at them to see how their craziness was going, being curious instead to see Bix's momma. Most of the people were so old I cruised right by them when checking to find her. I only had my sight of her at the baseball game, in her black dress and her hair full of wind bouncing up and down, and I almost did not recognize her when I passed my eye by her. In fact, if it had not been for the stepfather coming up beside her bed and bending over and saying something to her, I would have kept looking. She was that different.

You would have sworn this person never could have been the one at the game and done the things she was doing, jumping around and clapping and digging her boy while he played baseball. This life was so different, and she looked like she belonged here, and had never lived anywhere else.

She was lying back on her bed and looking over our way, smiling very slightly and not especially alert. Bix was watching too, and stepped into the room. Her eyes lit on him, like everybody else's in the room, and all of them looked the same as hers and her face did not change one iota when she saw him. This gave me the quick creeps. Maybe I am wrong though, I thought—maybe I just can't recognize her expressions.

Her hair was flat and waxy, no shine. Her face was skinny now but even so there was enough flesh to sag on the bones in it, though the color was gone from what flesh there was left. The skin around her eyes was tight, and slightly darker in color, like she had not slept for years. The eyes looked out at you and you saw they were deep, but there was nothing behind them, only just an empty room far away waiting to be filled up with whatever fell in front of the gaze. That is how it struck me, at least. To Bix I think it looked much different. After all, it was his momma. But I would never have said that person on the bed was anybody's momma, and for sure not that she was watching her boy walk into the room.

Everybody watched him take a few slow steps. They all stopped whatever they were doing and stared, completely quiet, looking slightly curious but like they expected no answers. Bix took a few more steps and then stopped. He was almost at the foot of her bed now. He reached into his coat pocket and pulled out a handful of clover flowers tied together with a piece of green ribbon. They were pretty beat up, but he looked down and tried to spruce them a little bit. Then he looked back up and locked eyes with his mother and just stared at her, not moving.

What happened then was very fast and very magic, the kind of thing you don't believe you saw and convince yourself was not so right away, but the fact is I saw it and I understood it, very clearly. Right there, on Bix's face, like a movie run a thousand times faster than the scenes it shot, I saw him go through every one of the strange changes he had made in the past six months. His face showed every single one very clearly for just one second, BAM an expression that I could not miss as the pie in Home Ec, BAM an expression of playing bounceball alone in the dark, BAM whipping his stepfather, BAM BAM BAM, so fast that anybody else would think he was just twisting his face. I knew exactly, though I cannot say why. I recognized those twists and I saw what he was doing with them, or, better to say, what was being done to him: He was taking care of every one of those changes for the last time, and then letting them go, one by one, gone forever. BAM he felt each one twinge for the last time and it flew off him and he was free of it. So, when it was over, he was left standing there at the foot of his mother's bed completely clean, free, and ready to start something new. He said in the car about his glove, this was always the first day, and here it was. He could now do whatever he had to.

He looked fresh and better than I ever saw him, and he felt it too, for now he beamed at his momma. They had stared at each other the whole time he went through his numbers, but her expression had not changed much, only the smile getting a bit more curious. But he smiled big now, and almost laughed he felt so good. He lifted the flowers, leaned forward on his toes to take his first step at her and you could see the word coming to his mouth and he enjoyed feeling it come, poised there about to run to her and call her Mother. But while he hung for the very last second before this, his last moment of fresh and silent, his mother opened her mouth and spoke first. Very clearly no mistaking it, in a nice calm voice, she said:

Whose little boy are you?

Whose . . . For a second everything froze in that room. I checked it out like I was the only one left free to look around. Bix was hanging on his toes leaning straight at her, his mouth open, his eyes right in hers. She was looking at him peaceful and expectant, smiling almost politely, and you could see that what Bix must have thought was love so strong it kept her from speaking was really plain curiosity and not very much of that, for on every face in the room, watching him, the same expression hung. The stepfather was watching Bix and he was the only person hip to what was going on, looking very worried and not sure he could do anything, which he couldn't, any more than me.

Then things broke and went back into motion and things had to start happening now. I had just had time to see what I thought was going to happen—Bix stumbling and trying to stop, his mother confused, everybody getting wise, Bix losing everything, his momma getting just enough to go crazier than ever before, and bad thing after bad thing all because she waited to speak until he was on his way to

her. I almost turned away not wanting to
see it bust loose. But now I am glad I did
not turn away, for I would have missed the
greatest single move in history, and I would
have missed my last sight of Bix too.

What Bix did was, out of nowhere, pull
the fastest and completest fake possible,
and pull it on thirty people instead of the
usual one. Here is what he did: Just at that
last tip of a moment before he fell off his
toes on the run to his momma, he snapped
his feet and somehow eased his body and
when he came down with his weight
instead of charging at his momma he
angled straight off, with barely a jag, for
the bed next to hers down the line, very
clean, perfect, strong. His momentum took
him right there and he switched his eyes
right with his direction, staring with his
big smile now right at this old scared
woman lying on that next bed, an old thing
too old to be anybody's mother, watching
him come out of the corner of her eyes and
pulling her covers up under her chin,
saying Oh goodness, oh oh oh. No one would
have ever believed this was Bix's momma
but his move was so great he pulled it off,
coming to a stop with his feet at the side of
her bed, but keeping up the lunge of his
body and throwing himself onto her,
arms flying around her neck and squeezing
her into him as he buried his face in her

neck and hair and sobbed out so loud we all could hear, MOTHER MOTHER MOTHER.

Oh, the old woman said, straining her neck around to get some air as Bix squeezed her harder and the clover he had in his fist under her chin got into her mouth. Oh oh my, oh.

MOTHER, he said, from his chest, sagging onto her old body with his weight now, because his back was shaking bad and his legs could not stand him up completely as he shook and cried. MOTHER. He shook and squeezed and pulled at the old woman, pressing her and boring his head into her neck. She wrung her neck around and her eyes spun scared like a dog hit by a car.

Everybody else thought this was just wonderful, including Bix's mother behind him. Every one of the patients watched this beautiful reunion with big smiles, and they nodded every time Bix sobbed MOTHER and looked quick at each other like they all were so glad to know things were so right. Bix's mother was gladder than anyone else, for she was the first one to speak.

Look, she said to her husband beside her, look—he loves his mommy.

Yes, said the man.

Oh my goodness, said the old woman, as Bix jerked at her and wailed into her neck.

But Hazel does not recognize him, said Bix's momma. She frowned a little. It's sad, you see.

Yes, said the stepfather.

Oh, said Hazel, hands plucking, neck wringing. Bix sobbed more slowly now, running out of it.

It's . . . see? said his mother, frowning, getting unsure. He loves her . . . But her voice changed a little when she said it and she broke off frowning deeper, with a question in her somewhere all of a sudden. Bix heard the change, and he reacted. He swallowed his crying down, and shook off the shakes, and took a deep breath pulling away from Hazel's neck. Hazel did not jerk away but just lay there watching from the corner of her eyes, not at all sure it was ending. Bix left his hands on her as he stood up, slowly, straightening himself up all the way, but keeping his back to his mother completely. Hazel plucked and pulled at her covers but said nothing. Bix's mother was watching, but frowning and puzzling now.

Bix looked down at Hazel. She watched, scared, whispering Oh oh very faint like if he did not hear her he would go away. But he reached his hands out and took her face in them, and he bent straight at the waist and gave her a big long gentle kiss on her face. Then he stood up straight again, dropped his hands back to his side and said, in a clear voice everyone could hear: Good-bye, Mother.

Nobody said a word. He stood for a second. Everybody watched him. Then, very slightly, keeping his back to his mother, never giving her another look at his face, he turned and walked up the lane beside Hazel's bed and out into the aisle. His head was turned away from the direction he came, and I could barely see the edge of it. He hung for just a second there at the foot of the bed, looking down the aisle the other way to the far end, and then he turned very neatly and started walking there. I looked past him and saw a door just like the one I was standing in. He was going away.

Still nobody spoke. We all watched and listened to his steps, very even and slow. He kept himself straight and walked directly down the middle. As he passed each foot of the bed, each person gaped at him and then watched his back, turning their head slowly as he moved on. He was probably halfway there the first time his mother spoke.

But . . . he is going, she said, shaking her head like she knew somehow this was not the way it should be. Bix hesitated for a half step when he heard her but he did not turn around. He even picked up the pace a little. It was a race, after all. He had the moves but she was thinking as fast as she could, frowning and rubbing her face and looking very intelligent indeed just then, no craziness but just someone feeling a very delicate mistake deep somewhere and going through everything until it is found. Her husband stood there looking down at her and then up at Bix's back as he moved further away. The dude could do nothing—he could not help her remember or help her forget, and probably he was not sure which he wanted her to do anyway. He just looked back and forth, wondering like me and like Bix if the kid would make that door before it hit.

There is . . . She shook her head hard and mumbled like to get dirt out of a shoe. It did not help. She was not there yet. But Bix almost was. He was just passing the last bed.

All of a sudden, just as he pulled even with the last edge and had ten more feet of open floor, something happened. An old crazy person, so wrinkled and flat you could not tell man or woman, jumped out from behind the bed and stood smack in his way, grinning scary and eyes wild, holding out both arms like to grab the boy and hold him there forever. I went tight and cold because I knew he had no time left and now I wanted him to make it, and he would not.

This old crazy would snag him and it would all break open and fly loose.

But Bix took care of it, this was nothing compared to the move he was pulling, nothing at all—he snapped a quick head fake at the old thing and the crazy went for it, jumping to the left and reaching with the arms, but by then Bix had stepped past and now he was in the doorway and the old person leaned on its bed and was the only one in the room not staring at Bix's back, straight and small in the doorway.

He stood there for two seconds. I don't know if he was waiting to see if she would get it and call him back at the last second, or if he was just giving us our chance to say good-bye, but that is just what I did. I stood straight in the dark on my side of my doorway, and I held up my hand and said See you, Bix, in a whisper nobody heard but me. As soon as I had said it, and as soon as his mother shook her head harder than ever and put her hands over her eyes, he slipped off to the side so quick I could not say which way he went. He was gone. It was good-bye to Braxton Rivers the Third.

One minute there was Bix and the next there was not. I suddenly remembered myself, and I felt myself there, standing alone in the dark just outside a door to a room full of crazy people. Watching Bix until he vanished—that is just what I always did, wasn't it? I stood outside Bix's door where it was a little crazy inside and I watched. Man, when I thought of it there like that, I hurt. I felt like for the first time in my life I had failed at something. For the first time, there was a thing I could not get just by trying hard and wanting it—I could not get into Bix. I could watch, like everybody else. I could squeeze into every space in his life I saw, and pay every bit of attention, and always be there for him to see if he ever looked around, but he did not. In some ways the dude was not born with eyes, but was like a bat, feeling everything by vibration and reacting to things we could not see, spinning and stopping and sidestepping like there were ghosts in between us people.

I hurt especially bad because I had to stand there and watch Bix pull off his finest number, and I could not be close to him or part of it. For that move he pulled on his mother and the crazies, that was not just another weird spot of jiving. It was the best thing Bix had tried to do since I knew him. It did not work perfectly, it was maybe not completely right if you had time now to think it all out, but at the heart he had tried to save everyone some pain.

It was good he was quick. He did not beat his mother by much. As soon as he was gone she commenced to shake her head harder and harder and make little half words in her throat, holding her hands to her mouth, eyes smart and racing. Then all of a sudden she stopped moving completely. Her face went long, her hands dropped. Her eyes saw it all right there at the foot of her bed and her mouth fell open and strained to say the name. She jerked up in bed and whipped her eyes at the door he had gone through and she got it all, but too late, the name coming last, but she had it now and she cut loose with it in the wildest scream I have ever heard, BIIIXXXXX. She threw out her arms at the door and leaned her face to it and shrieked it, BIIIIIXXXXX BIIIIIIXXXXX. All the patients fell back into their pillows and a few even wailed scared but she was clear now and she even knew she was too late. BIIIIXXXX she screamed like someone was killing her, and she decided to follow him and thrashed her arms and legs out of the covers, BIIIIXXXX BIIIIIXXXX BIIIIXXXXX, wild and fast flinging herself out of the tangle of sheets. But her husband decided to stop her and grabbed at her to hold her on the bed. BIIIIXXXXX. She turned completely wild when she felt him grab her, throwing her arms out at the door and then whirling them backwards and out to the sides, swinging her legs hard up and out, twisting and bucking and snarling and whipping

every part of herself as far as she could, till
you could see he could not hold her and so I
ran in to help.

She was screaming so loud I clapped my
hands over my ears at first but forced them
down so I could grab her, blinking there
while her things snapped around me and
not knowing what to go for. I made a snatch
at her left arm but I did not go rough
enough for she jerked it away and I chased
it, falling across her just as she cut loose
with a BIIIIIXXXX against my ear and I
fell back with my hands up to my head.
This was a mistake. Her left knee whipped
back and caught me in the ribs, knocking
my breath out, and I dropped my hands to
my stomach, only one second before her left
arm whipped back from where I chased it
and the elbow smacked me full force right
between the eyes. That was all for Jerome.

It knocked me back off the bed flat
against the wall and I cracked my head
hard backwards. For a second everything
fizzed and went silent and white, then I got
my sight back in time to see three worried
dudes running over in green pajamas
though not the black dude, and two of them
had big leather belts and the other had a
shot needle. My hearing did not come back
all the way though, for the last thing I
heard was BIIIIIXXXX but fading like I
was speeding away quite fast. I felt myself

sliding down the wall and thought I would never hit bottom, and on the way down everything just went white on me.

28.

There is nothing more for certain about
Bix. Nobody saw him again. His stepfather
called the police as soon as Bix's mother
was quieted down which took a while, and
they told him to check the train and bus,
and we went, but first they had to give me
a couple head x-rays because of my bumps
But I said it was okay and we went, just a
big ache and very sore between the eyes. At
the train station we found a lady who sold
a ticket to a kid for the train that just left
for Washington DC. She didn't see the kid
get on the train but she said he sounded
something like Bix only not dressed up, but
Bix would have been smart enough to
throw away his red tie if he wanted to
switch from one outfit to unnoticeable plain
clothes.

I did not believe he had run away that
far, but only because he had left his glove.
After all that work and all that thing meant
to him I couldn't see it. But I was wrong. He

did run away. Maybe he did not plan on needing it, maybe he was truly going to start something fresh, and there would be no gloves in his new life.

We went to the bus station but nobody had seen a kid and no bus had left in the last hour or so, and nothing else was leaving that night except for going southeast and then on down to Savannah. This bus would stop in Wilmington, and we decided I would go on it. Bix's stepfather wanted to leave right away to chase the DC train and maybe beat it to Washington and see if Bix got off and catch him. He asked me if Bix ever said anything about wanting to go to Washington. I said I didn't know. The stepfather looked at me like maybe I was hiding something. If I had known anything, I probably would have hid it, for though I had not had time to think about everything and evaluate all the angles, it seemed if Bix wanted to get away maybe he was right to, and somehow it did not feel bad and desperate and dangerous like it would with some kids. It was strange and sad, but frankly Bix running was so much less strange and sad than all of the other things I had seen in the past couple of hours and week that it was more like relief. It might even have been a good thing, who knows? Maybe the only place for Bix was away. I hated losing him right then but even so I felt these things. However, his stepfather did not, he was going nuts trying to figure out how to get Bix back and he did not think any of the angles I did. I suppose he had his side. It is pretty bad to lose a kid like that especially when so many things have just happened and you want to explain them and you think if only the kid could hear you explain them he would not run.

Then there was Bix's mother, and I know the stepfather was torn up over what this would do to her. I did not even want to think about where this thing had put her back to, or what she would have to face if she ever did get well. But the stepfather had to think about it, and I guess he was pretty scared.

Whatever all the reasons were, we had a pretty bad fight there at the bus station. He said I should hide and see if Bix came for the south bus which stopped in Wilmington and maybe he wanted to sneak back to the house or something. I said I would wait for the bus but not hide, and he said Would I call the cops to get Bix and keep him? and I said I would not do such a thing, never. If I saw Bix I would talk to him but that was it.

Well, the dude blew up at me, and started accusing me of things, and pretty soon he had worked up all kinds of jive, like Bix running was half my fault and like I influenced him the night before with the help of my momma to run away, and pretty soon he was telling me I had planned the whole thing with Bix and was there just for decoy and I was supposed to have kept him occupied while Bix got away and that was why I faked being knocked out and had head x-rays and all such trash as that. He got screaming at me, and I got screaming at him, and he like to hit me and I would have jabbed him too, but by that time several big black dudes had heard us and came out of the baggage room and stood tall and got a little tough with the stepfather and he got madder and nobler and put everything down to me, and he said one last thing to me, he told me Don't think I don't understand you, boy, and don't think you did Bix any good at all with all of your black-cat basketball and your black-cat fakes. See where faking got him?

The black dudes did not take kindly to this talk and they grabbed at the man but he jerked away and walked back to his car and left me for the bus. I did not have the money but one of the black men got me on free.

I was pretty cool that night on the way back but when I got to town and called Momma and Maurice borrowed a car and picked me up I got upset. I broke down pretty bad, and it was worse because I had a headache and worst of all I was starting to wonder myself what I had given Bix and where it was likely to get him? and all of it so confusing to me. For once, Maurice was not the child head doctor. He was just my brother and he pulled no jive, just drove me out and parked near Catalpa Park and we just sat there while I blew it out, him listening and saying things once in a while, all of them gentle and direct and not meaning very much but making me get calm. I got home and was too beat to tell Momma much but I guess Mo did, for the next day she and I talked a little but really we just did not bring things up very far, because I did not want to and told her I would think about things and just get back to normal. I STILL haven't talked.

I had headaches, and so I got more x-rays and they found a crack in my head somewhere and I missed the whole rest of the school year except for the last two weeks, nearly one month of classes, but I did work at home and slept a lot and still got all A's except in Phys Ed. I got no grade in Home Ec but they gave me credit. I deserved it, ask Henri and Mo.

Then it was summer and no sign of Bix and I decided to write this book. Now it is fall and you have the story.

But I have something, too. It came in the mail the day before yesterday. Only I saw it, nobody else, and nobody ever will. It is a postcard. It came addressed to me in printed letters. On the front is a color photograph of the Capitol building in Washington DC. On the back the message spot is blank. There is only my address.

There are some people on the steps of the Capitol. I looked at them through a magnifying glass but could not find him and I doubt that is why he would have sent it anyway, but I just wanted to check. I could probably not find him in Washington any easier. Nobody could, not with the tricks he was starting to pull. He could find his way in that city and lose his way for everyone else, and he could make sure of his secrets every step. That is what this card says, plain as if it was written in ink right there where is says MESSAGE HERE.

Maybe you are wondering why I am not all touched and tender at how he thought of me in the middle of all his trouble, how he cared to let me know about him, took the risk somebody might turn the card over to his stepfather and so on. Why aren't I all soft and mellow and full of good teary jive? Well, you think about it. Then you think about the way he whupped his stepfather, about the pie he brought to my family, about the moves he laid on everyone in that loony ward, from Hazel to his momma. Now you see? This postcard—sure, it might be the tender Bix reaching out to let me know; but it also might just be the next in a long line of great fakes, baby, and from now on with that dude you got to watch your step and cannot go feeling anything too fast.

I got my own fakes to worry about now. I have not played ball since Bix ran away. Are my moves gone? I doubt it. But I will find out tonight. My head is healed up and the nights are getting cooler and everybody is still full of baseball and summer jive, so they won't notice old Jerome slip out in the dark with his lantern and slide across the marsh and vanish into the forest. Then it will be just Jerome and Spin Light and we will see what we can see and there will be nobody else, not for a long time indeed.

But even though I will be out there by myself I know one fact from now on, one thing I have picked up from this whole story of Bix and me and seeing how things you start and stop so neatly by yourself do not always end on the spot. The fact is—if you are faking, somebody is taking. This is true for me, juking through the woods with my ball, and for Bix, cutting through the streets of DC with his life. If nobody else is there to take the fake, then for good or bad a part of your own self will follow it.

There are no moves you truly make alone.

Large print edition design by Marci Siegel
Cover illustration by Wayne Winfield
Composed in 16/18 pt. New Century Schoolbook
Printing and binding by Braun-Brumfield, Inc.,
Ann Arbor, Michigan